D1569925

"There's A Small Hotel" *Séjour du septembre 2014 - voyage en amoureux.*

This was about our 10th stay at Hotel Eber Mars. We have been staying there since 1990, before Jean-Marc Eber became owner. The location is superb, the rooms nicely refurbished, and the staff great (especially Jean-Marc who can advise on anything from Restaurants to which bus to catch). There is a book written about the hotel (part fiction with the names of people changed...but you know exactly who she is talking about) by Elizabeth Cooke, an American who spends several months a year at the hotel, and who we believe is writing a second one. Do try to get your hands on this book, as it perfectly captures the ambience of the hotel, the neighbourhood and the characters who stay there. A good read.

Trip Advisor, France

"A Tale of Two Hotels" is the fourth and final volume in the series about the Hotel Marcel, a small hotel in the city of Paris. Each of the four books represents a visit the narrator, Elizabeth, makes to Hotel Marcel, and include: "There's a Small Hotel," a sojourn in October; "Secrets of a Small Hotel," the following month of May: "The Hotel Next Door," Christmas and New Year's, later that same year; and finally, "A Tale of Two Hotels," which takes place the subsequent May.

The series is the author's love letter to the Hotel Marcel, and to the city of Paris, for the joy they provide, the mystery, the idiosyncrasies of personality, the poignancy of love, the lilt of melody, the taste and scent of extraordinary *cuisine*, and the gift of feeling at one with the world.

Many more positive reviews have been expressed about the series:

"Marvelous. I am ready and eager for the "Small Hotel" sequel. Great Fun."

Peter Gates

"So delightful, so evocative of the city the quartier, the hotel, your friend, M. Eber. Your adventures are like stepping into a light hearted French film."

Mary Ellin Barrett

"Wonderful..."

Nancy Regensburg

"Just read "Secrets", I loved the book."

Peter Gates

"Can't wait to read your next installment of your engrossing Paris series!"

Claudia Wasserman

"The book is really fun, impatient to know what was going to happen next in "Secrets." Strong narrative drive, one of your gifts as a writer."

Mary Ellin Barrett

BOOKS BY ELIZABETH COOKE

LIFE SAVORS
EYE OF THE BEHOLDER
A SHADOW ROMANCE
THERE'S A SMALL HOTEL
SECRETS OF A SMALL HOTEL
THE HOTEL NEXT DOOR
A TALE OF TWO HOTELS

A Tale

of

Two Hotels

ELIZABETH COOKE

Elizabeth Cooke

abbott press

A TALE OF TWO HOTELS is a work of fiction. Names,
characters, places and incidents are products of the author's
imagination or are used fictitiously. Any resemblance to actual events,
locales, or persons, living or dead is entirely coincidental.

Abbott Press books may be ordered through booksellers or by contacting:

Abbott Press
1663 Liberty Drive
Bloomington, IN 47403
www.abbottpress.com
Phone: 1 (866) 697-5310

Because of the dynamic nature of the Internet, any web addresses or
links contained in this book may have changed since publication and
may no longer be valid. The views expressed in this work are solely those
of the author and do not necessarily reflect the views of the publisher,
and the publisher hereby disclaims any responsibility for them.

Any people depicted in stock imagery provided by Thinkstock are
models, and such images are being used for illustrative purposes only.
Certain stock imagery © Thinkstock.

ISBN: 978-1-4582-1876-6 (sc)
ISBN: 978-1-4582-1878-0 (hc)
ISBN: 978-1-4582-1877-3 (e)

Library of Congress Control Number: 2015935113

Print information available on the last page.

Abbott Press rev. date: 03/17/2015

PROLOGUE

IT WAS THE best of hotels, the Hotel Marcel, a pocketsize essence of France.

It was the worst of hotels, the Hotel Majestic, a behemoth of anonymous overkill.

The two hotels, side by side, cheek by jowl, on one of the more elegant boulevards in all of the capital city of Paris, present a rivalry of taste, amenities, experience and clientele.

And I am on my way to witness the duel between them, because there must be competition in play, a war of sorts between David and Goliath.

On this return trip to Paris – another adventure to be had in the month of May – on the plane itself, before arriving at de Gaulle airport, I mentally review my previous visit, the most recent of many. It has been only four months since I was last in Paris. During last Christmas and New Year, a dramatic, delicious, exciting time was had, leaving me with so many unresolved endings to love affairs, to animosities, to longstanding friendships. Included in my reminiscence, is the opening of the new monstrous intrusion, the hotel directly next to Hotel Marcel, The Majestic, a five-star, white facade on the placid avenue.

However, in my memory list of the last visit, and most important, was the discovery of new love in my life – my Paris artist and long distance love, Ludwig Turner, (called Brit, because his mother was an English lady.) For us both, an elderly romance began, each of us in our 60s. I am astonished that no other love has inspired me as much as this one: no marriage paper is needed; no kids to worry about; only long, slow love that defies age.

No wonder I am beyond eager to return; love to be lived and a war of hotels to be witnessed! Who could ask for more? And after all, the excitement transpires in the City of Light, in the light of the world, Paris.

Oh yes, I am keen to be in Paris for other reasons as well – to return to the scene of the crime? I don't mean that literally. At least, there has not been a newly minted wrongdoing in the last months of which I am aware.

However, during my earlier October sojourn, eight months ago, one night, I saw a murder in an apartment across the avenue. On another, I saw a dinner party where a brute threw himself across a dining table and broke it in half. I saw an African-American find his French father, a white bourgeois gentleman, and perform as bass player in a nightclub called Le Club. I saw that same young musician find love with a beautiful girl, named Lilith, wearing a burka, who happened to be trying to shed that constriction. I saw an American photographer, working in Paris, mount many a model because he left the blinds of his window wide open in his duplex on the other side of the street. Ah, and so much more.

And this 'viewing' was all from the balcony of my room on the fifth floor of the Hotel Marcel, my favorite small hotel in all the world. Opposite, across the avenue, the three apartment buildings and their lighted interiors at night, provided the stage for the above dramas, and I relish the thought of having the opportunity to revisit that theater again.

And now, the Hotel Majestic, a resplendent endroit, has been built directly next door to Hotel Marcel. How is that affecting my small hotel? How does Jean-Luc Marcel, the owner/hotelier cope with this gigantic operation, a mightily unbalanced competition?

He HAS to have survived and flourished because for me the Hotel Marcel is a place where I feel so totally in my own skin, where Jean-Luc Marcel, has become a trusted friend, where The Eiffel Tower lends its strength and glow to the *quartier* and where the true Paris, with all its charm and joy, just happens to reside.

CHAPTER ONE

J'arrive á L'Hôtel Marcel

WALKING INTO THE Hotel Marcel, this Friday morning in May, having been driven here by Mounir, the driver who met me at de Gaulle airport, as arranged by Jean-Luc Marcel himself, I feel like I am coming home. Well, not exactly home, but to an exotic, sensuous, delicious place where I feel truly myself more intensely than any other venue. Perhaps because I lived in Paris when I was young, there is an emotional recall.

Behind the check-in desk, Brigitte, the Scandinavian *femme de chambre* is posted. She comes from around the desk towards me with a "Welcome, Madame Elizabeth." We hug each other briefly. "Monsieur is back in his office," but I see him rushing towards me through the small hall in the rear of the building. He too embraces me at the entrance of the lobby,

"Ah, Elizabeth. You're here once more," Jean-Luc exclaims happily. "Your suite is ready!"

My 'suite' is a small, tidy bedroom and bath on the fifth floor of Hotel Marcel, with a balcony that provides visual access to the life of the residents across the street. How I relish the thought of using my binoculars, actually a present from Jean-Luc when he discovered my secret vice of optically eavesdropping on those poor souls across the avenue, and seeing if all is as I remember.

Jean-Luc is helping Mounir, the driver, bring in my bags from the street, as he chatters away with animation. "You know I bought the apartment across the street – finally! That Louise Croix – she cut a hard bargain, but Isabella and I are there now. You must come over tomorrow and see what she has done with the place – around drinks time?"

"I'll be meeting Brit."

"Bring him! I really like your artist friend. Later, we'll go to dinner. Okay?"

"*Bien sûr,*" I say with a smile. "*Et merci,* Jean-Luc. I have to hear about all the changes that have taken place during these past four months."

"Oh my. There have been a few. Besides the new apartment, well, let's see. I am losing Antoine – you know, my night man."

"Oh no," I say, picking up my carry-on bag. "He is so nice."

"Yes, but he is just finishing up at University and is going back home to Alsace."

I move toward the entrance door and hand Mounir his euros – with a healthy tip.

"I love you, Madame," the little fellow says with a huge grin. "I love your money!" (He always says this to me. It is 'our' joke.)

"And are there more changes, Jean-Luc?" I ask, walking back to the elevator near the door to his office.

"There are a few," he calls from the lobby desk. "We'll get to all that. I know you're tired, Madame."

"I'm exhausted. Later, I'm just going to run across to *La Terrasse* and get one of their delicious cheese omelets," I call to him, as I wait for the contraption to descend.

As Brigitte climbs up the circular stair to the fifth floor with my two bags, and I squeeze myself into the tiny *ascenseur,* I hear the sound of a familiar voice. It is that of René Poignal speaking with Jean-Luc up front. I realize that the intrepid French detective has become a friend of my hotelier, but he also has been active in the resolution of more than one problem in the neighborhood. I wonder just what this visit might be about.

How exciting! René Poignal is always accompanied with drama.

Ah. At last. The pristine bed. The welcome bathroom with its glass shower. The French doors. The balcony overlooking the avenue below and the apartments across the street. Above all, The Eiffel Tower in all its grandeur, standing tall against the sky. How blissful. I'm home.

After a phone call to Brit, where the sound of his voice sends me into a dream of delight, our arrangement for tomorrow evening cemented, and a loving, steamy goodbye, "*à demain*, my love," *à demain*, I lie down on the pillows with a sigh.

I rest a while. I do not nap. I decide to unpack, which I do neatly. I am hungry. I descend in the *ascenseur* (which is claustrophobic to say the least,) and walk up the avenue and across a boulevard to *La Terrasse*, where I am cordially greeted. (I often have eaten here. I am an old customer.) I order their *omelette au fromage*, a *non pareil* delicacy, rich and creamy, paired with ideal *frites* and a glass of *Merlot*. Now, how can anything be more delightful; only the thought of my little bed in the Hotel Marcel where I can sleep away airline fatigue and dream of a tomorrow night with Brit in my arms.

CHAPTER TWO

Jean-Luc and Isabella At Home on a Saturday Afternoon

IT IS HARD to believe the difference in the apartment building 2 duplex on the fourth and fifth floors, the digs of Sasha, my American photographer friend first, then, art forger, Jillian Spenser and her young daughter, Amelia, and most recently, occupied by the original owners, Louise and Edouard Croix. Now, at last, the property belongs to my eminent hotelier, Jean-Luc Marcel with his beautiful consort, Isabella.

And the place is transformed.

The Croix pair had left the apartment empty but for two ancient, dark green sofas, a dark green side chair and a battered wooden side table. Isabella has had the sofas recovered in a vibrant yellow, the side chair in a gray and white print. The table is refinished in a honey color, the floorboards painted a pale gray, walls dead white.

On the table, I notice a copy of French *Vogue*. The cover model, of course, is Lilith, the Qatari girl, (beloved of Duke Davis.) This is the infamous issue that has caused huge comment. It is a stunning picture. She is beautiful, with a tendril of her ebony hair coiled in a curlicue of the Eiffel Tower stanchion, her bare toes touching a mound of snow. No wonder she has become such a sensation because the pose, her face, the concept is so unique.

I have come to Jean-Luc's duplex for an early evening cocktail reunion of sorts. Housed across the street at Hotel Marcel, in my fifth floor balcony room, I can glance across to see within Jean-Luc's new domicile, but only part way, of course. Now, here in his apartment, I am enclosed in the charming *décor* and warm welcome of my hosts. All is lovely.

I stand in the window next to Jean-Luc. We look out over his balcony with its two pots of bright, red carnations, gleaming in the late afternoon May sunshine. Across the avenue, the two hotels are side by side, the small, intimate Hotel Marcel, dwarfed by the large, white, elaborate Majestic. I am struck by the different perspective this view of the pair of buildings elicits, a view that colors the whole.

I look up at the royal suite balcony where Lilith resided last Christmastime, where Duke Pierre Davis, my African-American young friend watched and longed for her, from his attic room above this very apartment, my Romeo and Juliet lovers, now divided and lost. How sweet a couple.

Jean-Luc looks at me. "Quite a sight, the two," he says.

"You mean Duke and Lilith?"

"No." He looks surprised. "No, I'm speaking of the two hotels. The great, white whale, The Majestic, and the little brown minnow, my Hotel Marcel, side by side." He chuckles. "It is *très interessant* that my hotel is 96 % full; the other, just about 48%."

"No!" I exclaim. "That's fabulous. You were right, Jean-Luc. Hotel Marcel has a true Parisian ambiance that The Majestic cannot possibly replicate. And look at the Majestic – not one – but two doormen in front of that grand entrance, with gold epaulets on their uniforms. Gold, yet! That's new and, I'm sorry, but that's reaching!"

Jean-Luc laughs and hugs me. As we turn into the salon, I notice, hanging by a leather strap on a peg by the door, a pair of large binoculars.

"Well, well, Jean-Luc. I see you have taken up my vice," I say, pointing to the voyeuristic contraption. "I brought mine with me, of course. My balcony over there," I say, indicating the Hotel Marcel, "wouldn't be as enticing without the power of enlargement!"

If a Frenchman can blush, Monsieur Jean-Luc Marcel does so at this moment.

"I appreciate that enlargement," he says with a shy smile, slightly embarrassed. I nod, and smile back.

Isabella is in the kitchenette preparing luscious figs wrapped in *prosciuto*, chunks of *parmigiano reggiano* in a glass dish, and a bowl of *kalamata* black olives, which she brings to the side table. She and I sit on the yellow sofa, while Jean-Luc goes to the refrigerator, and brings forth a cold bottle of *Sauvignon Blanc*. He also selects three stemmed glasses from a glassware *armoire*.

"Madame Elizabeth, welcome home," he says with delight. The three of us lift our drinks and toast each other.

"There is nowhere else I'd rather be," I say, knowing that in minutes, my Brit will walk through the door. He is to join us for dinner – (and me, for the remainder of the night.) What a delicious way to return to Paris, as I have yesterday, Friday, arriving from New York. I plan another three blissful, adventurous weeks in this elegant city that I so worship, with people about whom I care so much, (some more than others.) What challenges and delights await.

Is Duke back from Qatar? Has anyone seen Lilith? And Sylvie LaGrange? Is the good doctor Guillaume Paxière bedding her? Or has he transferred his affections (and body) to Elise Frontenac? There are so many tangled tales to sort out and conclusions to discover. These fill me with excitement and curiosity.

There is a tap on the door. It is he. Ludwig Turner, my Brit, my artist love of some months now, tall, gray haired, lean in his black jeans, and joyful at the sight of me as I run to his arms.

After affectionate greetings on all sides, the four of us decide to attack the *Fusion* dining room of The Majestic – "just to test it out," says Brit. "It might be fun to see what they come up with, with their expensive Japanese chef and high and mighty manner."

"Let's do it," I say, and we repair across the street and through the heavy doors to the lobby of the grand hotel.

It has not changed since I was here last, four months ago, at Christmastime. The large black and white lobby floor is still slippery and shiny, and Nelson, the manager, presides behind the marble-topped check-in-desk as is his wont. When he sees us, he gives a supercilious nod of recognition and turns his back abruptly.

The dining room, named *Fusion*, is brightly lit, with white linen on each table, a votive candle in the center of each. The chairs are black leather. The waiters' outfits exactly match this cold *décor*, the whole effect evoking a penguin-like association, which I remark upon. Jean-Luc cannot help but chuckle.

Seated, we pore over the heavy, black leather menus, presented by a waiter from England. His accent is pure cockney and in fact, he is hard to understand. Brit engages him and discovers his name is Blakely and that he's from Liverpool. Blakely recommends the scallops as being particularly fresh.

I choose this dish. Jean-Luc and Isabella decide on selections from the Sushi menu and Brit orders a *steak/frites*, because, he says, "I want to see if *Fusion* offers anything remotely French."

In fact, it is the only item presented to us that has any connection to a French dinner. My scallops are laid out on a plate in a wide circle, each of the six, separate, at the edge of the rim. Although nicely browned and appetizing looking, they are cold. In the center of my plate, is a brownish, pink sauce of indeterminate flavor (although it is listed as 'pomegranate reduction' on the menu.)

Jean-Luc's and Isabella's sushi are the most elaborately arranged morsels any of us has ever seen, with carrot sticks up-ended, sesame seeds spread about, a sprinkle of black truffles, and drizzles of wasabi sauce over all. Jean-Luc insists that it tastes all right, but I notice Isabella is poking at the food in front of her with a tiny fork. Only Brit lucks out, in that his steak is rare, as ordered, (if a bit tough,) and the *frites* are crisp.

After secret smiles and sarcastic remarks passed in undertones, we order a selection of desserts from a rolling wagon. Well! You have never seen such a display. It makes *Le Nôtre's* classic array look positively simple in comparison. Mounds of chocolate *ganache* covered with bright, red maraschino cherries; purple grapes atop a *tarte au citron* covered in whipped cream and hazelnuts; flakes of coconut dusting a *crème brûlée,* which I choose because it looks the simplest. The crust is properly crusty, the custard beneath ice cold.

And the bill for all this? Don't even ask!

As we leave, our waiter, Blakely, asks Jean-Luc in his nasal voice, if indeed, he is the owner of the hotel next door.

"*Mais, oui,*" Jean-Luc replies, pleased at being so identified. "It is a hotel much less grand than this," he says, deprecatingly, "but I believe it is truly a little piece of Paris." With that, Jean-Luc looks about the anonymous dining room with something like contempt.

"Ah, Monsieur," Blakely remarks. "That must be…a relief!" And he gives a great sigh, at which we all laugh, including Blakely. "By the way, when you come in again, ask for me. Ask for Willie. That's my name."

"We will, Willie," Jean-Luc says. "And you must come by to see how the other half lives." More laughs all around, (and a good monetary tip, from Jean-Luc to his new friend.)

We roll out of there in high good humor after a very poor meal but more than sufficient vintage wine. We go perhaps a few yards, and enter the warmth of Hotel Marcel's salon and a delightful bottle of *Grand Marnier* provided by the owner which the four of us down until the wee hours, exchanging jokes and endearments happily all the way, and so glad to be together. In Paris!

And for me and Brit, especially glad to be together – finally – alone on the fifth floor of the Hotel Marcel with the glow of The Eiffel Tower shining through the open glass doors to my balcony.

CHAPTER THREE

Where is Lilith? Where is She?

THIS IS THE question I pose, not only to Jean-Luc, but to Sasha, the photographer from the U.S., and Ray Guild, American Editor of French *Vogue*.

"Wish I knew," they each echo.

"I do know that the *Vogue* cover was a smash," claims Ray, lifting a cup of *café au lait* to his lips. "An absolute sell-out, for us. Everyone wants her, wants to know who the hell this exotic young beauty is. I even had a call from the advertising director at *L'Oréal*, wanting her to be 'the face' for their new cosmetics' line – would even name it after her – so of course, they wanted her actual name."

"Did you give it?" I say, suspiciously.

"Absolutely not. I kept my word to keep her identity a secret," Ray says in hurt tones. "I promised her anonymity and I kept that promise." He turns away from me.

"I have too, have protected her identity," Sasha interjects. "I have had more tweets and inquiry about the pictures of Lilith clinging to The

Eiffel Tower in my book "*Les Façades de Paris*" than I've ever had, even more than some of my most gory war photographs, in Syria, in Iraq. It's unbelievable the amount of interest…"

"Okay," I say. "I get it. The fashion world is clamoring for our Lilith. Isabella told me, that even at the Yves St. Laurent atelier where she works, they would love to get Lilith as their runway model."

"And Chanel has called me at *Vogue*, looking for her name," interrupts Ray.

"They find her delicate features and mobile expressions captivating…"

"And that small-boned body, so different from the average, pretty little model," Sasha chimes in with a lascivious look.

"Well, you would surely know about that, Sasha," I say with a laugh.

"No, but really," he continues. "There is something so provocative, in spite of the innocence she projects, an innocence, I might add, that is genuine." He looks at me seriously. "I mean it."

"But our Lilith has disappeared, returned, unwillingly, back to Qatar," I say with a sigh.

"Yep," says Ray. "Back to dear old Qatar."

"And under the thumb of that father of hers, Hamad al-Boudi. I'm sure he has her locked in a closet," I exclaim.

"Wonder if 'Howdy Doody' or whatever his name is, has seen any of her pictures," our photographer friend remarks.

"Oh, Sasha, really," I say. "Howdy Doody indeed!"

"You know me," he remarks. "Can't help it. But a scene between Lilith and 'big-daddy' would make for quite a show, I would imagine. How about no burka! How about the fact that her bare toes are touching the snow, in the Eiffel Tower picture."

"Oh, God," I say. "Bare toes. Anything bare is blasphemous."

The three of us have been finishing breakfast this Sunday morning. I had called them each yesterday, the day after my arrival (and before the passionate Saturday night with Brit,) to see if we could have a late Sunday brunch at the Hotel Marcel. Jean-Luc is, of course, across the street in his new digs with Isabella. He does not come to work on the weekends, unless there is an emergency.

So it is Sasha, Ray, and I who devour the fresh, warm *croissants*, and sweet, Normandy butter, wedges of *gruyère* cheese and apricot preserves and Greek yogurt with a lemony tang. Sasha even has two pitchers of hot chocolate, foaming and aromatic, instead of the usual *café au lait*.

"And Duke, my young African-American friend?" I inquire.

"He's back," says Sasha.

"When?" I am not surprised. His adventure to retrieve Lilith from Qatar had seemed something of a fool's errand, if a wistful one. "When did he return?"

"I guess he was only in Qatar maybe for a week or two."

"Did he see Lilith?" I ask eagerly.

"That I don't know," says Ray. "Do you, Sasha?"

"I don't know but I don't think so. He seemed really sad when he first got back."

"Where is he living?"

"Same place," says Sasha.

"The attic room, above Jean-Luc's duplex?" I am pleasantly relieved to hear this. Duke is nearby. That means I will see him, *bien sûr*.

They both nod. Then Sasha says, "He's back working at *Le Club*. You know, the jazz place up near the Boulevard Raspail?"

"I know it well," I say with a sigh. "What say we go together to hear him one evening…my treat?"

"Sounds good to me…Oh yeah. Let's go, the three of us," they say, speaking over each other. "Maybe we can learn something about Lilith."

"Say when," I exclaim.

"Tomorrow night? You think?" says Sasha.

"I know he used to be featured on Tuesdays and Thursdays, when he first started," I say, thoughtfully. "Perhaps we should make it Tuesday. What do you think?"

"Works for me," says the one.

"Works for me too," says the other.

And the deal is set for Tuesday night around 9:00 o'clock when I will reconnect with, Duke Pierre Davis, son (illegitimate) of Pierre

Frontenac, who resides with wife Elise, in apartment building 3, across the street, on the fourth and fifth floors. I hope all is well with father and son and step-mom. It had seemed smooth when I left after Christmas, but who knows what the New Year has wrought?

CHAPTER FOUR

René Poignal

IT IS BREAKFAST as usual on Monday morning, the wonderful warm *croissants*, the *café au lait*, brimming in a giant cup. I am relishing every morsel, the taste memory, reinforced and confirmed. I see from my vantage point at the front end of the salon table, the formidable figure, in trench coat – even though it is a warm day in May – of the local policeman, René Poignal.

He glances my way, and with a loud, "Madame Elizabeth," comes towards me with arms open. "How grand to see you again," and he plops across from me on an empty chair.

"*Bonjour*, Monsieur detective," I say with a smile. "Yes, I am in my favorite place in the world once again. Tell me, what is new and exciting on this street of dreams?"

"*Eh bien*, things are quiet – at least compared to the days of murder and confrontation with the *bestial* Kurt who 'did-in' his brother-in-law, Emile LaGrange." It always amuses me how René quotes American phrases because he is addicted to "Law and Order" which appears on

French television. "Yes, it's quieter today," he continues, "but there are still *petits drames* among the residents on the street."

"*Quels drames?*" I question.

"Well, you know Sylvie LaGrange, the grieving widow?"

I nod.

"She has become involved, since Emile was murdered. There is this new man in Sylvie's life – a Dr. Guillaume Paxière."

"Hmm," I say. I know him well, the original roué, preying on wealthy, older women. (He had even tried ME, at one time, to no avail.) "Is Sylvie still 'the one'?" I inquire.

"It's getting *compliqué*, because the good doctor is also pursuing Elise Frontenac, at the other end of the avenue, and her husband is quite concerned."

"And Sylvie must be upset?"

"Huh! You put it mildly. She is enraged, of course. She hates the Frontenac woman. Sylvie is, as you Americans say, 'a loose cannon.' Also, she has a violent streak – as does her brother, Kurt, of course, but at least he's in jail. I have to be very watchful of the two women, and of course *le docteur*," he adds in a conspiratorial voice.

"Has anything happened between the two ladies?" I am deeply curious. I know both women involved. One I like and admire, Elise Frontenac. The other, Sylvie, I genuinely fear. She is a frightening, red-haired virago, loud and overbearing.

"Indeed, yes," René replies. "Last week, I saw them together on the street. It was raining and Sylvie LaGrange had her umbrella, not over her head, but in her hand, shaking the *parapluie* in the face of poor Madame Frontenac. It was positively menacing. I went over to the two of them. '*Vous avez un problème?*' I asked. Madame Frontenac was embarrassed, but that LaGrange woman, well, she just...*elle me moque.*"

"She sneered at you?"

"Exactly. Sylvie LaGrange is definitely someone to, as you say, keep one's eyes on."

I have to smile.

Jean-Luc joins us from his check-in desk. The lobby is empty, except, suddenly I see the cockney waiter…what was his name?…oh, yes, Willie Blakely, from the *Fusion* dining room at The Majestic. He enters and looks about hesitantly. He sees Jean-Luc sitting at the table with René and myself and approaches us cautiously, literally hat in hand.

"Ah, Monsieur," he says to Jean-Luc.

"It's Willie Blakely, no?" Jean-Luc responds.

"Yes, t'is," Willie says, smiling broadly, happy that he is remembered.

Jean-Luc rises and draws the man over toward the front desk, away from us. I can hear the mumble of conversation, when out of the blue, there is an outburst of laughter from Jean-Luc.

"Monsieur Willie," he says. "I cannot understand your French. That cockney accent. It's hilarious."

Willie Blakely is laughing too. "I know, sir," he says in English. "Can't help it. Best speak English, no?"

I see Jean-Luc nod vigorously.

Willie continues, in his nasal voice, "It's like this, Moseer Marcel. My dinner wait-shift in the *Fusion* dining room is from 6:00 to 10:00. Sometimes it runs later a bit, and often, I have to deliver room service upstairs. I also work from 7:00 to 11:00 in the morning, for breakfasts, again more room service," this said with a sigh.

"You're a busy man, Willie."

"I giss so, but not busy enough. I need…ya know…extra money. I have a tiny place in St. Germain, where I live, but it's expensive, and it's hard to get over there. It's a long way on the metro. I have Sunday and Monday when I'm off. See, it's Monday today, and I'm here now and for a reason," Willie says, with a little 'tada' gesture.

"Yes, it is Monday," Jean-Luc remarks kindly.

"Well, I need more work. I'm wondering if you could use a helping hand, sir?" he says, voice beseeching.

Jean-Luc is unprepared for this.

"I mean," Willie goes on, "I could be your night man, at least a late night man, for the people who come into the hotel in the wee hours. Or maybe from 11:00 in the morning, I could be at the desk. I know my French ain't that good." Willie pauses, quite breathless.

Well, I'll be darned! Willie is asking Jean-Luc for a job.

Jean-Luc has his hand under his chin, in a characteristic thoughtful pose.

"Well, Willie. I don't know. I am losing my night man in a few weeks. If you could only get here about 10:00 at night, well, that means I'd have to cover the earlier part of the evening. Hmm. Let me think about it. You could nap downstairs, when it's not busy up front. There is a bed there and bathroom, and of course a doorbell at the front entrance that rings down there, so you could be available for late comers."

"Oh my sir, that would be greatly convenient," Willie says hopefully. "Right next door. That would be my dream job. And I could be on the desk sometimes even earlier than 11:00 in the AM." His dark eyes are bright with excitement.

"Well, Willie, I'll have to see," Jean-Luc says. "Tomorrow morning, I'll come into the Majestic for breakfast and let you know. I like you, Willie. You seem like a decent man."

"Thank you, sir, *Merci bocoo*," Willie says, delighted with the possibility of a stint at the Hotel Marcel. "This is such a…sweet…place." And he bows out, walking backward through the lobby door. "*À demane*, Monsieur Marcel," Willie calls goodbye in his 'unusual' French.

"*À demain*, Willie." Jean-Luc pauses a minute, then joins us at the salon breakfast table.

"Well, what do you know?" I exclaim.

"He's not a bad fellow, Willie Blakely. I quite like him."

"I can check him out for you, if you like," René suggests.

"*Bonne idée*," responds Jean-Luc. "You know, it may be a fine thing to have him here. He could provide a kind of liaison, a way of finding out, what goes on at the hotel next door."

"Another little spy? Like our Madame Elizabeth?" says René, glancing at me with a smile. "I assume you have your binoculars with you as usual."

I laugh. "Guess who gave them to me! Jean-Luc himself. And guess who has a pair of his own so that he can spy on his own hotel from across the street."

We are all laughing by now.

"Jean-Luc," I say. "Shouldn't you warn poor Willie that it's possible for Nelson or a bodyguard to come into the Hotel Marcel. He could lose his job at The Majestic – for being a traitor."

"I suppose I should warn him, but I do need a man. He's reliable, decent, polite." Then with an engaging grin, Jean-Luc says, "Besides, he can give me gossip on the activities over there, keep me up on the competition. Now that's worth the risk. And if Willie, should be fired, maybe I'll use him full time!"

"If he checks out," warns René

"*Absolument.* If he checks out."

Ah. A new fly in the ointment!

CHAPTER FIVE

Le Club

IT IS LATE when I descend on Tuesday morning. Brigitte is again manning the front desk.

"Where is Monsieur Marcel," I ask.

Her response? "He has an early morning breakfast meeting."

Ah, yes, I recall. Jean-Luc planned to meet Willie at The Majestic to hire him – or not. I have a feeling it will be the former.

Brigitte leaves her post to bring me my usual morning repast. My mood is aglow for tonight I am going to *Le Club* to hear and see Duke Davis. Brit, Sasha, Ray and myself will go over to the jazz *boîte* around 9:00 PM. I have told all three that I want a few moments alone with Duke, during one of the set breaks. He might be more forthcoming about his Qatar adventure and the status with Lilith (if any) just speaking with me and not facing a barrage of gentlemen asking questions.

They have all agreed to remove themselves for a smoke outside on the street at the given moment.

As I finish my first cup of *café au lait*, Jean-Luc enters the lobby, flushed and looking very pleased with himself. He comes right over to me at the salon table. There are three other Hotel Marcel residents finishing up their breakfasts too, each planning the day of tourism in Paris ahead of them, but Jean-Luc makes no effort to restrain his ebullience.

"He's on," he says, blithely. "He waited on me at my solitary table and we were able to strike a deal. He will start next Friday morning – 11:00 to 5:00 –then he goes to The Majestic from 6:00PM to 10:00 – then back here for the night. He has to be at the hotel next door at 7:00 the next morning for their breakfast service."

"Whew!" I say. "He'll be exhausted."

"Oh, he's a wiry fellow. Besides he needs the money."

"You're not waiting for René to check him out?"

"I told Willie that the job was on a temporary basis – a kind of trial period, to see if it works for both of us. That'll give René some time to explore *l'histoire de* Monsieur Willie Blakely."

"Makes sense," I say, downing the last drop of coffee in its massive cup. "By the way, I am going tonight to *Le Club* to hear Duke. Brit, Sasha, and Ray are joining me. Want to come with Isabella?"

"Not tonight, Elizabeth, but soon. I love the way he plays. I haven't talked much to him about his Qatar trip since his return. Of course, he's living upstairs over my duplex in the attic studio room, *comme avant*."

"I haven't seen him either, thus far in my few days here, although I look across to his room. The top half of the attic door is firmly closed. I hadn't even realized he was back there."

"Yes, he's been home in that room for several weeks," Jean-Luc says.

"Can't wait 'til tonight. I hope I get a chance to find out what happened in Qatar. I wonder if he even got a chance to speak to Lilith." I am determined that tonight will bring some answers.

"I doubt that he did," says Jean-Luc matter-of-factly. "He seemed really *triste* when he got back."

After this short exchange, I go upstairs and call my great friend, the American born Marquise de Chevigny – Sue – an old and dear *amie*, from our days in New York City when we were young. We have had delightful reunions since, here in Paris, and at her *château* in Montoire, some kilometers South of the capital.

We agree to lunch on the following Friday at *Caviar Kaspia,* our favorite haunt for caviar, vodka, and blinis, on a comfortable banquette, with Russian music playing, and long, heartfelt, gossipy conversation possible.

"*À vendredi,* sweetheart. Can't wait to see you," are her final words as she rings off.

Restless, I go to the balcony, binoculars in hand. I look across the street.

All is quiet in the three buildings opposite, blinds closed, and Duke's door at the top of Jean-Luc's building 2, is shut. One wouldn't know anyone was there. Even the front windows of the Frontenac's apartment, in building 3, are shuttered, strange on a sunny day.

I while away the afternoon, walking over to The Eiffel Tower, strolling through the Champ de Mars, conversing with the small, leashed Parisian dogs that abound with their masters in the park in the month of May. I find a *crêpe* stand and eat the delicious, sugary pancake, as thin as a wafer, warm and satisfying, as I sit on a bench in the shade of the tower. It is Paris at its most serene and I am replete.

The 9:00 PM hour approaches. I am anxious, as I shower and change into a white sheath with dark green linen jacket. I wear the diamond ear studs Brit gave me last New Year's Eve, always a crowning touch imbued with love.

I am not hungry, but in his office downstairs, I find Jean-Luc who offers me a glass of *Merlot* and some tinned cheese biscuits.

"Anything new with René?" I ask, as I sit in his cluttered place of business. He has turned on his computer to play music. (Jean-Luc is a fanatical jazz and rhythm and blues *afficianado*.) Right now, it is Miles Davis' mournful cornet that fills the room.

Jean-Luc shakes his head. "But Poignal is waiting for a major rupture between the two ladies on the street, Sylvie LaGrange…"

"And Elise Frontenac," I finish for him. As I say this, Sasha enters breathless.

"I just saw her," he bellows.

"Saw who?" Jean-Luc has risen from his seat behind the desk.

"Elise Frontenac. She was crying. She had a black eye."

So Paris isn't always so serene on a sunny day in May.

More *Merlot* is poured. Ray arrives, as does Brit, *mon amour*, and the three men Sasha, Ray, Brit – and me, leave quickly to find a taxi to take us to *Le Club* on Boulevard Raspail.

As we go down the stairs to enter the *boîte*, I hear the wail of a saxophone, pleading in a kind of anguish, the melody intoning the song 'Georgia on My mind.' In the club, we find a table for four near the entrance door. Duke is on the stage, plucking the strings of his bass. He looks older, to me, but still as handsome as ever. He does not notice us, so deep in the music is he. Another song is played, this time more upbeat – 'Sweet Georgia Brown' - and the audience in the crowded room claps along with the beat.

The set is over. I stand, as Duke sets aside his bass and walks to the front of the small stage. He puts his hand to his eyes, the better to see, then recognizes me, and with a broad smile, jumps down to the dance floor and wends his way through the tables to my side.

"Elizabeth," he says, embracing me, almost falling into my arms.

"Ah, Duke. I've missed you," I say. "Come sit a minute."

He pulls up a chair and does so, saying easy hellos to my three companions. We speak in generalities, when Sasha remarks that he would like a cigarette, and the three decide to go outside to smoke, (as prearranged, leaving me alone to speak with Duke.)

When they have gone, I turn to my young friend and say, "Tell me about Qatar. What happened there? Duke, I need to know."

He looks at me for a long minute. Then, with a sigh, he begins.

CHAPTER SIX

Qatar

"BEFORE I LEFT Paris, I bought a white Arab robe and a head covering, as well – you know, the white cloth with black cord an Arab man wears to secure it to his head? It was only about 18 euros for both."

"Where did you find these things?"

"In an Islamic bookstore, of all places. They had them there for sale."

"Did you ever actually wear this outfit?"

"Yes. When I got to Qatar, to the capital, Doha, I found a studio apartment for $159 a week. No lease, no credit check. I put my robe on there and the headpiece and walked the Corniche, a kind of waterfront promenade on the West Bay Lagoon of Doha. There is a park, Al Bidda Park, opposite the water, a lovely place, would have been perfect to have a picnic there with Lilith." Duke looks down, subdued.

"Did anyone bother you? Or think you looked...odd?"

"No. Not at all. You know, there are some darker skinned Arabs," Duke says with a sly grin.

"I know. I didn't mean that. It's just, that it was so bold. I must say it's amazing."

"What is?"

"Your courage."

Duke smiles again. "That was only the beginning, until I ran out of money," he says ruefully. "I found out where the family lives. Hamad al-Boudi is pretty well known. It was a great palace, all white, like The Majestic – in The Pearl Qatar – the most expensive part of Doha. I walked there, past the huge gates many times. I walked very obviously, in my robes, so Lilith might see me. I positively sauntered," he says with a smile."

"Did you ever see Lilith?" I ask softly.

"I did. Once. She was in a limo and the gates opened and the car emerged. I saw her in the window as the car passed. Her eyes met mine. She turned abruptly and looked about to faint. I know she knew it was me," he says sadly.

"Did you ever speak?"

"No...well not exactly...but we did communicate. I read in the newspaper, the social section, that Lilith was guest of honor at a function raising money for a children's hospital. It was on a particular night at The Metropole Hotel in downtown Doha. Apparently, Lilith does volunteer work at the hospital. Anyway, the day after the event, I bought a bouquet of beautiful flowers, cost a fortune, and I attached a card in an envelope, saying, 'Congratulations for a wonderful job' and signed it, 'an admirer from Paris.' In the envelope I put the little gold key I had given her, a key to a life we would share. She had sent it back in a love letter before being banished by her father from Paris."

"I remember. You said it was a kind of code for the two of you."

"Exactly. A code."

"She must have <u>really</u> fainted when she received that!"

"If she ever got it. I delivered the bouquet myself, when the gates were opened as her father left in his limousine. I was in my robe and head cover and went to the front door and..."

"You must have been nervous."

"My heart was beating so hard I thought I might faint," Duke says with a little laugh. "Anyway, a woman servant took the flowers. I knew enough Arabic to say, 'For Miss Lilith,' and the woman nodded and smiled and said she would take them right up to her."

"And then?" I am breathless with his story.

"Well, there's not much more to tell. I pray she found the key. She can reattach it to the gold chain I gave her and wear it next to her heart, if she still wants to." His shoulders droop, as do the corners of his mouth. "Of course, I still have the little gold box you gave me to put the key in. It's the other half of the code. It's right here," and he pats his left breast pocket over his heart.

"You didn't hear…?"

"There was no way. Besides, I was out of money so I came back."

"To Paris." I pause. Then I ask, "was it worth it, going to Qatar?"

"It was. Absolutely! She knows I'm still there for her, if she got the key, and if she can escape." Duke says this with a sigh. He rises. "Anyway, here I am again playing music at *Le Club*. They were glad to see me, thank God. I have the old gig back. I'm so glad you came tonight, Elizabeth – with your friend Brit - and the others."

"Me too. Me too," I say with conviction. "I must go join them outside in a minute, but tell me, your father, is he okay with your trip?"

"He's delighted I got home safe. Doesn't understand why I went, but you know, he's cool. Doesn't ask too many questions."

"And Elise?"

"She's okay with me, I guess. But it's funny, there's something going on with her…between them…husband and wife."

"What do you mean?"

"Well, they seem, I don't know, very stiff together, and every time I'm over there, for dinner or a lunch, there's this doctor fellow hanging around and she well, she is flirting and coy and frankly, ridiculous."

"What does Pierre say, if anything?"

"Nothing. Nothing at all, but I can tell, it bothers him. A lot."

"The doctor's name wouldn't be Paxière, would it?"

"Why yes. As a matter of fact, it is Paxière. She calls him Guillaume."

Well, the good doctor is still in business! But where in this picture of lust does the widow, Sylvie LaGrange fit? I wonder. Fit to be tied! I'll just bet.

The piano man is beckoning to Duke to come back to the stage. As he leaves me, he says, "I have written a song for her. I'm going to play it now," and he turns on his heel, and jumps up, to join his musicians. Sasha, Ray, and Brit, who have been waiting in a corner by the door, seeing how immersed Duke and I have been in conversation, now return to the table and we settle down.

"He is going to play a song he wrote," I tell them as we watch Duke pick up his violin. He is joined on stage by the *petite chanteuse*, who occasionally sings with the quartet. All is quiet in the room. Duke announces, "We are going to perform a song I wrote for my lady love," as which the crowd responds by stamping feet and clinking glasses. Then, all quiets down once more.

Duke speaks again. He says just three words. "A Golden Key."

The melody on violin begins. It is haunting, the words even more so, as they pour from the Piaf-like singer, in a high sweet voice.

"A key of gold,
For you to hold,
A golden key,
To unlock me,
To live our lives,
For all to see,"

The music and voice continue in poignant longing, finishing with the words, 'A golden key." It is so typical of Duke, the sentiment expressed and the haunting violin. The crowd is mute, and touched by his earnest delivery.

And I am moved to tears.

CHAPTER SEVEN

Isabella

"ELIZABETH, COME LUNCH with me, can you? on Wednesday - tomorrow? There's a fine place right next to the Yves St. Laurent building, off avenue Marceau on the Right Bank. I have so much to tell you." Isabella had called me late Tuesday afternoon with her invitation.

Of course. Of course.

I meet her at the atelier Yves St. Laurent. It's a beautiful, soft May early afternoon. We walk around the corner to a small restaurant named *Le Champignon*, famous for its mushroom broth, its mushroom omelet, and the perfect *champignons sur crouton*, the *sautée*, in butter and wine, on toast points. I choose the latter for my *déjeuner* and it is delectable.

"Tell me, tell me, Isabella. All seems so well with you and Jean-Luc." She blushes. "We are very happy."

"And work? Are you still sewing upstairs in that special room, the workshop, for *appliqués* and sequins and *paillettes*, the special beauty treatments to embellish ladies' dresses and evening gowns? You are so skilled in this?"

"Yes. I'm still there but now I am head designer for such things," Isabella says with pride. "It's wonderful, exciting, fun."

"You must get paid more too."

She nods with a little blush. Then she says, "You know, the fashion house was looking to find Lilith. They thought her photo on the cover of French *Vogue* was so...so *épatant*."

"Striking?"

"Yes. Exactly. Striking. Stunning. They wanted her very much for runway work." Then suddenly she asks me, "Have you ever heard the new name in fashion 'Rashid?'"

"I can't say I have," I reply. "Rashid? Just one name?"

"Yes. He is a Muslim from Abu Dhabi. You know, The United Arab Emirates."

"What about him?"

"He has only been here in Paris for a couple of years but he's gaining quite a name for himself. He produces a kind of Islamic fashion, he calls a 'modest Muslim' fashion."

"You mean, real clothes, not burkas?" I say with a grin. "'Modest Muslim.' Hmm. Are his things somber or boring?"

"*Au contraire,*" Isabella responds. "Oh, he uses long sleeves and high necks, skirts, but also peplums, chiffon halters, beading and lace cutaways, and the fabric, '*haute batik*' we call it, in wonderful tones, jade, rose, crimson, sapphire. He uses elaborate draping and, oh, the headpieces. Some are exquisite."

"Sounds fascinating," I say, lapping up the final mushroom morsels in their elegant sauce and the last bit of crouton.

"It is he, Rashid, who is determined to find Lilith and use her for his collection," Isabella continues.

"What?" My fork hits the plate with a clatter. "He knows of Lilith?"

"Everyone does, Elizabeth. You have no idea what a sensation that cover of *Vogue* created."

"No, I guess I don't."

"Rashid feels that the West panics about Muslims as the 'Other.' The jihadization of young men or whatever, separates Islam from the Western world. This rift is always illustrated by a picture of a woman, wearing the hijab or abaya, shrouded in black. Rashid believes that fashion can change people's ideas of Islam"

"Do you think it can?" I ask, incredulous.

"Yes, in a way. For women, 'I shop, therefore I am like you.'"

I laugh. "You know, you have a point. I guess clothing is a common language. It can convey the message that Muslim women live in the same world as everyone else."

Over coffee, Isabella continues, "Rashid's clothes are really beautiful. He is influencing even some of our designers at Yves. There are slim jewel colored dresses, with perhaps a long different patterned jacket in bright color with a flowered hoody."

"Now you really sound like a '*fashionista*,'" I say with a smile. "Is he making any money? Is he <u>that</u> successful?"

"Well, apparently he's being bank-rolled by a Qatari man who lives here in Paris. In fact, I have met him, a rather creepy fellow. He came to the atelier, I think looking for models, if you know what I mean. He said he wanted to see the 'competition' for Rashid, but I think he was looking for girls."

"Sounds like a real charmer."

"He even flirted with me. I told Jean-Luc who was wildly jealous." Isabella is laughing with delight.

"I'm sure he was. Jean-Luc so adores you."

"Anyway, this Saud al-Alami fellow, - that's his name - he came in a regular Western suit, a well-cut one, I might add." She makes a face.

"You would notice that!" I say. "But tell me more about you and Jean-Luc. You like living in the new apartment?"

Isabella's whole expression changes. "I love it. We love it. I've never seen Jean-Luc so happy. He loves cooking on his new Cornu stove. He loves watching his hotel. He loves the fact that his clientele over there can use the garage belonging to our apartment building. He loves everything," she says, glowing.

"He loves <u>you</u>," I say, touching her hand.

Isabella nods, smiling shyly. "One of the reasons I wished to have lunch with you is because I want to ask you something."

"Of course," I say seriously.

"Jean-Luc." She pauses. "Well, we plan to get married."

"How wonderful," I interrupt, truly excited. "I knew it!"

"Yes, it is wonderful. I wanted to see if you would stand up for me, Elizabeth?"

I am taken aback. I gulp with pleasure. "Of course," I say without hesitation. "I would be honored."

"We plan for a week from this coming Friday. You know, we waited until we were sure you would be here for the great event"

"Oh," I say. "I am really touched." And I am.

"We are just going to the *Mairie*, the town hall. Then, we'll have a small reception in the apartment. Later, we go off for the week-end, but the real honeymoon, we're going to the south of France, even to Spain, later in June."

"Oh my dear," I say, genuinely emotional. "I couldn't be happier for both of you, and I can't imagine a more enchanting duty than to stand up for you at the town hall of Paris and give my blessing. Good heavens," I say. "I'll have to buy a new dress!" And with that we leave *Le Champignon*, round the corner to Yves St. Laurent and discover the perfect outfit for me to wear at the *Mairie*, a gorgeous cocktail dress in deep blue that is NOT 'modest Muslim!'

When I return with my treasured purchase to Hotel Marcel, I almost run into René Poignal who is speaking in hushed tones to Jean-Luc who sits behind his check-in desk, listening attentively to the detective. There is no one else in the lobby.

"*Mon Dieu*," Jean-Luc is saying, a look of shock upon his face.

"Duke Davis just happened to walk in on them," René says. "Pierre had given him a key so he'd feel it was a home for him. Anyway, Duke just stopped by yesterday afternoon to speak to his step-mother, Elise Frontenac, about a surprise birthday party he is planning for his father, and her, of course, at *Le Club*."

"Duke walked in on what?" I ask.

"You don't really want to know," the detective says.

"Oh yes I do," I rejoin. "What did he walk in on?"

René, shakes his head. "Ahem." There is a long pause. Then in a hushed voice, the policeman continues, "Duke walked into the salon and found Dr. Guillaume Paxière with his pants down and Elise, on the sofa, disheveled, blouse unbuttoned, and skirt slipped to the floor! Is that what you wanted to know?"

Not really.

CHAPTER EIGHT

A Grand Entrance

WHEN HAMAD AL-BOUDI arrives late Wednesday with his entourage, the Majestic Hotel springs into action. Nelson, the manager, is in command, ordering doormen and pageboys alike to take care of the group from Qatar. After all, the conglomerate owners of the Majestic are Qatari and Hamad al-Boudi is one of them.

First, the bodyguards, in dark suits, four in all, appear, after the chauffeur opens the door of the white, stretch limousine, releasing Hamad al-Boudi from its interior. Then three burka-clad women emerge, shrouded in cloth from head to toe, including the face veil, (illegal in France.)

One of them is smaller and thinner than the other two, obviously young. Lilith? Oh, I hope so. A bodyguard clutches her arm. Heads bowed, none of the women looks up.

All sweep into the entrance of the hotel whose large doors clang behind them definitively, swallowing them.

I watch this from my balcony. It has to be Lilith, although I can't really tell. Is she really back in town? Why would her father bring her here again when she had escaped his grasp so blatantly last Christmastime? Has he seen the cover of *Vogue*, with his daughter clinging to a foot of the Eiffel Tower, her body outlined against the metallic structure? Has he seen the pictures of Lilith, taken at the same photo shoot, by Sasha, that are featured in his book, *Les Façades de Paris*?

Why, oh why, would Hamad al-Boudi return with his only daughter to the place of her Islamic disgrace, after running about Paris without her burka, being filmed in outrageous poses? Does he have any inkling of her romance with the black music man from America named Duke Pierre Davis, who she has heard play jazz in a French nightspot called *Le Club*?

It is hard to fathom. But Thursday afternoon, I discover that Hamad al-Boudi has brought Lilith to Paris to meet her intended. The father has arranged a marriage for Lilith with a man, a confirmed bachelor, named Sheikh Saud al-Alami.

"No!" I exclaim. "I heard his name yesterday – from of all people, Isabella."

"He's nothing but a Qatari playboy," announces René Poignal.

René and I are in Jean-Luc's office, where the owner of Hotel Marcel sits behind his desk, leaning back in his chair. "You can say that again," Jean-Luc mutters.

According to René, al-Alami has been personally selected by Lilith's father to be her husband. It sickens me, not just for the loss of love with Duke, but who knows what kind of man this al-Alami person might be.

"How do you know this?" I demand of René. "Are you sure?"

"*Oui*, Madame," continues René. "I found out these things because I am a policeman. I have 'connections' even within The Majestic. It is my job to know things on this avenue." René sounds quite pompous in this response, which surprises me for he is a most practical man.

"Tell me more," I say in a subdued voice.

"Sheikh Saud al-Alami – called simply 'Saud' by his friends - lives in a magnificent *hôtel particulier*, a mansion on the Right Bank, near the Étoile. He's been there for the past four years."

"How old?" I ask.

"Oh, late 40s I would guess. He's a permanent bachelor at the moment," René responds.

"Does he do anything?" Jean-Luc inquires, "like work?" His voice is sarcastic.

"I gather he is a distant cousin of the current emir of Qatar who appointed him to buy art for the National Museum of Qatar, an immense building project in that Gulf country, of five show place museums in Doha, the capital, one of which is designed by I.M. Pei."

"Sounds pretty prestigious," I remark.

"Saud is also purchasing art for his own private collection, no end to oil money for the man. He buys from churches, galleries, and major family collections where there is no problem of authenticity. Quite a *luxe* life, I would say."

"Wow." Jean-Luc is on his feet. "No wonder Hamad al-Boudi has picked him for Lilith. But with Lilith's 'disgraceful' behavior, according to her father, why would Saud accept such 'tarnished goods?'"

"Well, according to of all people, our little Willie Blakley, Saud has been to dinner several times at the *Fusion* dining room at the Majestic. Always with a model and other friends. Willie has heard him talking about the picture he has seen of a beautiful Arab girl on the cover of *Vogue*, of how she is a work of art. He claims that it is time for him to marry, and is under pressure from his famous family to do just that. He wants to have her and keep her for himself as a prized acquisition."

"Ugh," I say. "Poor Lilith."

"Of course, al-Boudi is accepting of all this because Saud IS the emir's cousin, and perhaps he realizes that his daughter's physical exposure has in some way increased her value," Jean-Luc expounds.

"However," René continues, "according to Willie, the last time al-Boudi was in Paris, he ordered lots of room service with forbidden booze delivered by our cockney friend to his suite. Willie claims he is now bringing bottles of single-malt scotch, champagne, brandy to the sheikh practically on an hourly basis. The old *hypocrite*! His concern about Lilith is taking its toll." Jean-Luc starts to laugh at the thought.

"I thought booze was *verboten* for traditional Muslims," I interject.

"It is. But Saud is a blood cousin of the most powerful family in Qatar," René goes on, chuckling along with Jean-Luc. "So hypocrite or no, boozy evenings and unresolved thoughts, the power, the money, evidently they mean more to al-Boudi than does the happiness of his young daughter. But, in fact, the whole idea is making him quite sick."

This brings silence to the three of us. Finally, I ask, "What does Saud look like?"

"Oh, like an Arabian. He dresses in Western clothes, according to Willie, and he would know. Clothes made in London, Saville Row, but, apparently when he purchases art or is expected to perform things for the family, he wears the white robe and head covering with a black cord," René remarks. (À la Duke, I think, in his costume.)"Saud drives around in a Bentley. He is slender, somewhat effete, fancies a small thin moustache."

"You have seen him?" I ask.

"Madame, I am not a police detective for nothing. Of course I have seen him! I went over to his mansion to get a good look. You know, a situation like this, well, it can *s'enflammer*...you know, grow."

"Become enflamed?" I question.

"Exactly Madame. With power, money, certain rigid mores, beauty..."

"Sex!" adds Jean-Luc. "*C'est un cocktail explosif!*"

Lilith is back! And she is really in trouble. Duke must be told. And soon.

CHAPTER NINE

Caviar Kaspia

ON THIS BEAUTIFUL Friday, I arrive at our favorite meeting place, Sue's and mine, *Caviar Kaspia*. Every time I am in Paris, the two of us lunch here, to delight in the Tsarist Russian atmosphere and indulge in the best caviar in all of the city and, most important, delicious conversation.

I am first and am seated at a banquette in the corner of the upstairs restaurant; the walls, a soft green; the melody in the air from a balalaika. Sue appears, dressed in a chic, dark linen suit, with a small hat atop her upswept hair.

"You look marvelous," I say, rising and hugging her. We double air-kiss, and she sits down with a little laugh.

"You do too, sweetheart! And it's so wonderful to see you again after only four months. I think that's a record, even for you, to come back this soon."

"You know, I can't stay away. After all, Brit's here."

"And how is your artist lover?"

"We are very well together," I say, beaming. "He is planning to come to the States for the whole summer, to be with me out on Long Island. He loves being near the water."

"He loves being near you," she says wryly.

Sue settles back as we order the poached eggs, topped with caviar, and a carafe of iced vodka. "Tell me, tell me, how goes it on the avenue?"

"Oh, my goodness. There's so much going on. It's hard to know where to start."

"How about at the beginning."

"Well, you knew Duke Davis went to Qatar to retrieve his lady-love, Lilith," I begin.

Sue nods. "He really went?"

"He did. He didn't actually speak to her, but he was able to make his presence known to her. Anyway, he's back here in Paris, saddened but still determined. Lilith is back again too. Hamad al Boudi arrived late last Wednesday with entourage. He has lined the poor girl up, I understand, to marry a Qatari man who is living here in Paris."

"Oh no," Sue exclaims, taking a swift drink of cold vodka from her tiny shot glass.

"Perhaps you've heard of him," I say. "You get around. His name is Saud al-Alami."

"Not Saud!"

"You know him?"

"I've met him, more than once. He's kind of a sleazy character – very rich. Oh, he's a proper Muslim, but that doesn't stop him from being addicted to fast cars, pretty models and the bachelor life. He's not about to give all that up. He's to marry Lilith? Oh, poor child! I don't envy her."

"How did you come to meet him?"

"I guess, the first time at a party. Yes. A married couple, old friends of mine, they were in Paris for his leave. They are living in Qatar. He is a Major at the U.S. base there. Did you know that we have the largest military base in the Middle East in that aspiring Gulf emirate, good old Qatar?"

"No. I had no idea."

"Well, Saud came on to me pretty strong, although I'm much too old to really appeal to him. He likes young and nubile, but I think the title of Marquise got him. He was particularly impressed that I live in a *château*. That kind of thing has him talking to himself, if you know what I mean."

I have to laugh, and yet, it is hardly a laughing matter with Lilith's future hanging in the balance.

"What else is new?" Sue asks, between bites of the delectable soft egg with beads of briny caviar intermingled.

"Well, our friend Dr. Guillaume Paxière was literally caught with his pants down."

"What?" Sue squeals, laughing with delight. "You're kidding. Tell me. Tell me."

By this time, I am laughing too. Dr. Paxière is a man-about-town known to *tout Paris*. Sue has encountered him, and he was off and running after her madly. That *château* surely is a magnet, I thought, for a certain type of man-about-town. She had found him easy to dismiss, as had I, because the poor man's ego is so fragile.

"Apparently, Duke walked into the Frontenac apartment – he has a key because Pierre wants him to feel at home there. He came to speak to Elise about a surprise birthday party he wants to give for his father at *Le Club*."

"And…?" Sue is all ears.

"He came through the salon, and there was the doctor, willing and ready to climb aboard."

"Naked?"

"No, but a bit undone."

"And Elise?"

"Half undressed, I gather. She must have been shocked to see Duke."

"Did he say anything? Has he told his father?"

"Oh, I would doubt it. I don't think Duke wants to rock that boat, but I honestly don't know."

We are quiet a moment when Sue blurts out, "What about the merry widow down the street, the one you said Paxière was pursuing? What's her name?"

"Sylvie. Sylvie LaGrange." Again, I am laughing, unseemly or no. I can't help it. "For all we know, there'll be another murder on the block!"

"Yes. You told me Sylvie considers Doctor Guillaume Paxière to be her personal possession and hers alone."

"That's a laugh," I say. "That man belongs to no one!" and Sue and I set off on a round of girlish giggles, munching on *fraises des bois* with *crème fraiche*, and, and downing shot glasses of vodka, one after another.

CHAPTER TEN

Lilith's Fate

LILITH. SHE IS curled up in a chair in Jean-Luc's office. When I return from lunch with Sue, this Friday afternoon, one week after my arrival in Paris, Willie Blakely, now on duty at the desk, tells me in a loud whisper, to go back to Jean-Luc's office 'for a conference.'

"You sound so mysterious, Willie," I remark as I go back there directly. The door to the office is locked. Rare. I tap on it, saying my name, and Jean-Luc opens it and ushers me in throwing the bolt closed behind me.

Her burka is on the floor at her feet. She looks so little, so young, and there are circles beneath her eyes, but when she sees me, she jumps up and embraces me. "Oh Elizabeth," and tears are falling, from both of us.

Then, quietly, she begins her story. Hamad al-Boudi sees the *Vogue* cover. He sees the pictures in Sasha Goodwin's book, *Les Façades de Paris*. As Ray Guild predicted, Qatar is a sophisticated, wealthy country, aware of European mores and current passions.

Copies of Lilith's pictures were presented to Hamad al-Boudi from all sides, from enemy and friend alike.

"My father was furious. He would come to my room at home in The Pearl Qatar – the big house. Not only how dare I appear without a burka, in the picture on the cover of *Vogue*, but the fact my feet are bare and that my body is stretched against a metal foot of The Eiffel Tower, for all to see. Oh, oh," and Lilith cannot continue.

"You must have been afraid," I say gently.

"No. I was not afraid. Only a little," she admits. "I told my father that it is <u>he</u> who is afraid …of the world."

"How bold of you, Lilith," I say. "How brave."

"He responded 'I'm afraid for you daughter, of the world corrupting you.' That's what he said. 'The world is decadent, often indecent, dangerous.' Not all of it, I said. I was thinking of you, Elizabeth, and Monsieur Marcel… and my Duke. 'I am strong, father,' I told him."

"You are indeed," says Jean-Luc respectfully.

"'You may think you're strong, but you are young,' he said, so dismissively. I'm about to turn 20. 'Hah!' he said. 'Exactly! 20.' Then I told him I want to explore the world, the life I have been given. I don't want to be like so many of my friends, girls I have known since birth, who are to be married off in arranged marriages and live lives, each in obeisance to their husband/master. 'As well they should' was his response."

"I do not want that for me," Lilith continues, turning to me imploringly.

"'Please, father,' I said to him. 'Let me be different. Let me have a life to love and a love to live with. Otherwise I will die.'"

I am holding both her hands.

"Of course, he told me I was being dramatic. 'You shall have an arranged marriage. I am studying several possible men, with power and wealth, who will give you all you need, serious men.' I replied, 'who will have concubines just as you do!' I don't know how I was able to be so bold." Lilith shakes her head.

"I don't know either," I say.

"'How dare you,' he shrieked at me. I told him, the man will need me only for my fertility and when I have produced babies, he will be on to the next woman." Lilith's voice is bitter. "'You are a silly child,' he shouted. 'No, no, I tell you, I will die,' I shouted back."

"Oh, Lilith." Her story is so vivid.

"Then he got really serious with me. For the first time, I was truly frightened. 'Do not be so rebellious, daughter' he yelled. 'You will not die. But you will be punished. I see it is necessary to keep you deep in the house under surveillance and you will bend to my will.'"

Lilith stands. "'I will run away,' I said. He laughed. 'Ridiculous, my girl. Not only ridiculous, impossible!'"

Apparently, Hamad al-Boudi moved quickly out of the room, shutting the door firmly behind him. Lilith could hear him turn the lock before she gave way to tears.

She ran to the window. Below, in the garden she saw two of the bodyguards, Ahmed and Mounala. They were smoking, leaning against the white pillar next to the entrance door. In the driveway, a stretch limousine awaited Hamad al-Boudi's presence, to drive him to a conference in downtown Doha with a group of export/import men, interested in increasing the price of oil to the outside world. Oil is only one of the products al-Boudi has the right to export: pricey leather goods, woven rugs, grains. He is also a member of the conglomerate that owns a number of hotels in and around Europe, the latest being The Majestic in Paris.

"And now he brings me here to meet a man I must marry," Lilith murmurs, weeping full out. I put my arms around her as she sits crumpled in the chair.

When her sobs subside, and Kleenex has been applied to her face and eyes, I ask her, "Have you seen Duke?"

She shakes her head sorrowfully. "I haven't been able to," and she starts to cry again.

"I know he is waiting for you," I say, as softly as I can.

"We love each other." It is said so simply. "You know he came to Qatar to find me? I saw him once – he looked so funny in his Arab robes. I was in the limousine and our eyes met." Lilith smiles then starts to cry once more. "He sent me flowers and the golden key." She fingers the gold chain around her throat from which hangs the tiny symbol of their passion.

"He was desperate to find you," I tell her.

"Where is he?" she breathes.

"Right across the street in the same attic room," Jean-Luc says gently. "You can see him from your suite balcony, as before."

Her face lightens with a beautiful smile. "Will you tell him to look across to me?"

"Of course," Jean-Luc says. "Of course I'll tell him. He doesn't realize you're back in Paris."

"We will have to get you two together," I say.

"But how?" Lilith asks. "I was only able to sneak over here because of Mr. Willie. He took me downstairs by the servants' elevator in the hotel when my parents were out."

Thank God for Willie.

"Well, perhaps it can be done again," says Jean-Luc.

Lilith looks perplexed.

"The old buildings like those across the street, they too have servants' elevators at the back – you know from the old days, old ways. Perhaps we can take you up the servants' elevator at the back of my apartment to Duke's room."

Lilith rushes towards him. "Oh, Monsieur Marcel, If you could." Suddenly, her wan little face has become radiant. "Oh please, Monsieur, if you could," and this time she bursts into tears of joy.

As do I.

CHAPTER ELEVEN

Brit

I SEE WILLIE Blakely at the check-in desk in the lobby, this Saturday morning, on my way out to shop around the corner. It is a little after 11:00 AM, and I am off to *Le Nôtre* for some picnic supplies. Brit and I are going to lunch *en plein air* in the Bois de Boulogne on this balmy day. He is to pick me up around 12:30.

"I have to ask you, Willie," I say in a low voice. The lobby is empty at the moment. "Why did you bring Lilith to Jean-Luc – and more important, how?"

"I saw that poor girl. So sad. So restless. Every time I go to that suite, there she is, not allowed to go anywhere, and scairt of meeting her would-be mate." He shakes his head. "I feel sorry for her."

"Me too," I say. "But how did you manage to bring her here?"

"Well, the sheikh and one of his wives(?)" Willie's eyebrows make a question mark, "they be out and about. I was delivering new bottles of water to the suite and liquor – to all his suites – he took them all, the whole fifth floor -can you imagine? Anyway, she was there looking so wistful, staring across the street, poor little thing. I suggested she might want to go down with me, in her burka, a' course, and at least take a little walk around."

"You did?"

"She got all excited, and down we went in the back elevator, she head to toe covered, and she asks me if she could stop and see if Monsieur Marcel was in his office – and well, that's about it. You know the rest. Later, I took her back to The Majestic before 6:00, when my wait shift begins, the same way, in the elevator that room service uses at the back – you know, for trays and luggage and supplies for the upper rooms."

"Brilliant," I say. "You may have to repeat the process again very soon," I say, elated at the thought of bringing her across the street up the back elevator to Duke in apartment building 2!

"Anytime, Madame Elizabeth. Anytime that little one can escape, I'm ready."

I find a fresh, shrimp salad with herbs, a soft wedge of *Brie*, and a slice of *paté de campagne* in the cold case at *Le Nôtre*. With a *bouteille* of *Merlot*, a *baguette*, and a sac of multicolored *macarons*, my picnic is complete.

All I need are utensils and napkins, which Hotel Marcel will lend me. Perfect.

And it is perfect, the picnic. Brit has brought a blanket, which he spreads on the grass under a great tree. I distribute our delicious food, cutting the *baguette*, holding the wine glasses, which he fills. We sit happily together, looking at each other, laughing, touching. I tell him of the Lilith saga and the fact that we are hatching a plan to bring her to Duke's attic room for a reunion.

"Might be a bit dangerous for her," Brit suggests.

"We'll be very careful," I say. "But, you're right. Her father…"

"And mother, remember. She can't be too pleased with her daughter running about unescorted – and with a black man."

"They don't know about Duke."

"Not yet," Brit says. "You can try it – getting her up to Duke's place – but then, I think it might be better – safer – if you brought her to the

Marais – to my house. Duke and she could meet there. The sheikh would never think to go there, would he?"

"Oh, Brit. *Quelle idée!* What a marvelous thought. Thank you, darling, for being so romantic."

"Come here, you," he says, pulling me to him.

We go back to the Marais and spend the afternoon as lovers do. We decide to go this evening to *Le Club* and break the happy news to Duke that his Lilith is back in town. I can't wait to see his face.

We arrive by taxi at the Boulevard Raspail, walk down the side street to the staircase leading down to the entrance of *Le Club*. The jazz *boîte* is below street level, and as we descend, the blast of improvised sound rises to meet us.

Brit and I find a table for two, close to the bandstand. Duke looks down at us, and with a big smile, waves his left hand before reaching for the strings on his bass for the next song, 'Satin Doll.' We each raise a wine glass to salute him as the final notes end the set.

Duke jumps off the stage and pulls up a chair from an empty adjoining table.

"Elizabeth. Brit." He is beaming.

"You're at it again," Brit says. "The music. It's wonderful."

"Thanks," Duke says modestly, accepting a glass of wine. "It's what I do. I'm really grateful that they held my job here for me when I was in Qatar."

"Hey, Duke," I say, somewhat conspiratorially. "I have news."

"Oh?" Duke pricks up his ears. "About Lilith?'

"She's back."

"In Paris?" His voice rises.

"Yes, Duke. She's back at the Majestic."

"You're sure? Her father brought her back here? My God. I can't believe it." Duke is highly agitated. "You have seen her?"

I nod.

"How did she look? Is she okay? Did she mention me?"

I nod again.

"She more than mentioned you," Brit adds.

Duke relaxes a little. "I have to see her. Is she in the same suite?"

"Yes, she's there, looking across from her balcony. Looking for you."

"Oh, God." The young man before us is suddenly trembling, his mouth working. He sips some wine. "I have to see her," he keeps repeating.

"But why? How? Why did he bring her back to the Paris of her disgrace? I don't understand," Duke continues, regaining his composure.

"There's a reason," Brit says. "It's not good."

"What do you mean?"

"Hamad al-Boudi brought his daughter here to meet the man he has arranged for her to marry."

Duke is on his feet. The chair falls over. "What? He can't do that. This is not the dark ages!"

"Unfortunately, for some, it still is, Duke." Brit is trying to soften the blow.

"Look, maybe we can help, at least arrange a way for you to see her."

Duke picks up the chair and seats himself again. I see tears in his eyes.

"She can't marry someone else. She can't. I won't let it happen."

"Look," I say. "We have, I think, a way of bringing her up to your room."

"When? When?" There is hope in his gaze.

I explain to him the miracle of Willie Blakely, our cockney friend, who feels so sorry for Lilith, who realizes how unfair her situation, and who is more than willing to aid us in bringing the two *amants* together.

"God bless him," Duke says with a sigh. "Does she know of this 'plot?'"

"Yes," I say, smiling, "and she can't wait."

"Oh, God, when?"

I turn to Brit. "Willie's day off is tomorrow, Sunday. He has Monday, too, so how about one of those days. Perhaps he could bring her to you around midday, depending on what's going on with her family. You could have the afternoon together, at least."

"It's dangerous for her, Duke, but later, we might be able to bring her over to my place in the Marais district – you know, the Place des Vosges? The two of you could meet there," Brit remarks.

"Yes, Oh, yes! Anything." He looks down. "I can't tell you…" and he cannot speak. Then, he looks up. "Lilith, she means everything to me."

And I can see it in his eyes. True love is there hiding in the depths, and there is no doubt.

CHAPTER TWELVE

The Plot

DUKE IS IN the open upper half of the door to the attic room above Jean-Luc's duplex on this Sunday morning. He is looking longingly across the avenue to the balcony of The Majestic for Lilith's face and form. I notice as I step out on my own balcony, opposite Duke's building, that she is not there on hers, at the grand hotel next door.

Sasha had been in the room and balcony next to mine at Christmastime, but he has since moved out of the Hotel Marcel and found a little rental on the next avenue. Sasha, therefore, cannot take the kind of intimate pictures he took of Lilith four months ago when she had stepped out on her suite balcony, not anymore.

It is a lazy, hazy day, awaiting the rain. I go back into my room and prepare myself for the implementation of the 'plot.' As I enter the lobby downstairs, I see that Willie is there at his post at the check-in desk. There are no hotel clientele about, so I feel free to approach my co-conspirator about the possibility of taking Lilith to Duke's room across the street this very day.

"Might be a bit tricky," Willie says, *sotto voce*. "You know this is my Majestic day-off – so to reappear there – hmm, let me see. I could pretend I had forgotten me brolly – it's about to rain, ya can see – or some papers I need that I keep downstairs in my locker in the employee's room. Yes, that might work...look natural. Don't want to cause suspicion. That little fellow – the bodyguard – Ahmed – he eyes me funny from time to time."

"Yes, Willie. I think Ahmed is someone to be very wary of."

He nods vigorously. "I could call up to her suite – if she answers and no one of the family is around, she might be able to come down the back elevator – in her burka a course – and I could meet her and try to bring her over here. If someone else picks up...I'll just hang up."

"She could wait in my room while I contact Duke, Willie. I have his cell number."

"Okay. Let's try. But I can't leave yet," Willie says, looking at his watch. "Lessee – it's now about 11:30. I can get Brigitte to cover for me in an hour or so. Then I'll be on my way to rescue the little maid from Araby." And he grins broadly.

"I'm going over to *La Terrasse* for a bit of lunch. I'm starving. But I'll come straight back." And I take his hand and shake it.

I am excited as I cross over the next boulevard to *La Terrasse*. What Willie and I plan is dangerous for Lilith, I know, but somehow it's destiny speaking to me, and I am convinced it is the right and only thing to do. Our 'plot,' - conspirators, one and all – Duke, Lilith, Willie, Jean-Luc, Brit, me – we make quite a group – must succeed.

As I walk, I see Pierre Frontenac on the street. He is alone, head down, on his way, apparently, to his duplex apartment in building 3. I have not seen him since my arrival, and he does not notice me on the opposite side of the avenue. In fact, he doesn't notice much of anything, so preoccupied is he. I am struck by how thin he has become. I never thought him heavy, but now, in his light summer jacket, he appears much too slim for his stature. His clothes hang upon him.

I enter *La Terrasse* just as raindrops start to fall. I order a *salade Niçoise* – delicious – and eat quickly, my mind churning with thoughts of the afternoon ahead. In spite of the rain, which is more of a slight drizzle, I round the corner to *Le Nôtre* for a sac of their multicolored macaroons, and lo and behold, I see Henriette, holding a scarf over her head to protect against the drops, enter the store before me. She goes immediately to the cold case to inspect the display of salads, cold meats, and *oeufs mayonnaise*, to select dishes for the Frontenac Sunday supper, I assume.

I approach her, this *femme de ménage*, who I have come to know from dinners at the Frontenac's. Her acceptance of Duke, as Pierre Frontenac's son has impressed me. She is one of those rare, devoted personages who is true to her employers and feels a part of the family.

"Henriette," I say, as she peers into the depths of the cold case.

"Ah, Madame Elizabeth."

"Vous allez bien?" I ask.

Her face is troubled. "Not so good," she says mournfully. "Things not so good *chez nous.*"

"I'm sorry to hear that. I saw Monsieur *aujourdhui, sur la rue.* He looks *très mince.*"

Henriette nods. "He does not eat. Not at all." And her mouth droops. "It's that *docteur, toujours la bas. Il est méchant.*" She shakes her head vigorously.

Paxière! I am sure of it. He is always about, according to the good-natured *femme de mènage.* Elise is surely taking risks. And Pierre? Losing his appetite with good reason.

"Take care, Henriette. I hope to see you soon," and I leave her to retrieve my sac of cookies and return to Hotel Marcel in time for the adventure.

I ask Brigitte, the Swedish *femme de chambre*, who is covering for Willie at the desk, to tell Willie, on his return, that I am in my room and for him to call me there.

A call that never comes. Instead, within minutes of my return upstairs, there is a tap on my door and Willie, with Lilith, in dark burka trappings, are standing there in the tiny hall. She is partly wet with drizzle, but the smile on her face is one of sunlight and glee. She is the ravishing girl I recall.

"Come in. Come in," I say, and they do, Willie, looking shy and a bit uncomfortable. "Everything go okay?"

"Yes," he says. "I did run into Ahmed, near the back elevator. He asked why I was there. Fortunately, I had some papers in my hand that I told him I'd forgotten – rental papers, I said – and he left just in time before Miss Lilith came down in the elevator. Blimey, it was a near miss," Willie says, wiping his forehead.

"But I'm here," Lilith cries with delight. She sheds her burka, and in a suit of pale gray linen, she runs to my balcony and steps out. The rain is abating, but she still gets drops in her hair and a spattering on her jacket. She doesn't care. All she wants is to see Duke.

"Careful, Lilith," I call. "Step back. You don't want to be seen by everyone."

"Just Duke," she calls back, but she does retreat closer to the building.

Duke's attic door is open at the top, the half-door swung wide. I reach for the phone and give his cell number. I hear his voice. "Look across, Duke. She's here."

And suddenly, I hear a cry from Lilith. Duke is in his window, waving at her, his face wreathed in smiles. He beckons her, and she leans forward.

"Careful, Lilith." She does not respond. She is speechless, but I see she is nodding as Duke's door closes.

She runs to me. "Can we go? Can I go now?"

"I guess so. Willie, you take her to the back elevator of Duke's building. I'm sure he will be there to greet you both, to take her upstairs. Find out what time you should pick her up again and bring her here to me. She can put her burka back on and return to The Majestic."

I turn to Lilith. I take both her shoulders. "Darling girl. You must be very careful. It could be dangerous for you – and for Duke – if you are discovered."

"I know. I know." She is literally jumping up and down like a child.

"I wish there was some way to disguise you," I say.

"It's too warm for your old brown coat," she says with a little laugh. That coat of mine had helped disguise her on the cold winter streets last Christmas.

"I know," I say. I go to the *armoir* next to the bed and take out a black beret that I had bought as a present for a friend. It has the word 'Paris' in white letters across the brow. "Here, put this on, and I'll pull your hair back so it doesn't curl around your face as usual." I do just that, and it is astonishing how different Lilith's aspect is, except of course, the exquisite face is the same.

"Don't stay too long," I admonish the two, as she leaves with Willie.

"I'll never forget," she whispers to me, and they are off.

Whew! I'm a nervous wreck. I go to the balcony. As the sun begins to filter through the clouds, I see that Duke's upper half of the attic door is firmly closed.

Enough already, I think, as I sink down on the coverlet. And let us pray.

CHAPTER THIRTEEN

Angst

I CANNOT LEAVE my room. I am so anxious about the two, Lilith and Duke, across the street. I pace the small, bedroom area, go out on the balcony more than once, and find I have devoured almost the whole sac of *macarons*, purchased at *Le Nôtre* earlier this Sunday.

Lilith left with Willie almost two hours ago. In her black beret, with hair in a long tail down her back, she looked a Paris *gamine*, not a rich Arabic heiress. But one can never know the hands of fate, and all I can do is fret, and wait, and fret some more.

Her burka is folded neatly on my bed. I pat it from time to time. It is not soft, and the deep, dark color bothers me. So unfeminine, so much a shroud, so cold a garment is this piece of cloth, and heavy, cruel to wear.

Finally! Finally. The tap on my door, and Lilith stands before me. She carries the beret, and her hair is loose and lovely about her face, which glows, emitting a radiance that surrounds her.

She comes in shyly. Willie is nowhere to be seen. She sits on the bed, next to the burka, then, leans back, throwing her arms behind her, luxuriating in the softness.

"Lilith, Lilith," I say. "Did all go well? Did anyone see you?"

She nods happily, then sits up. "Duke met us. He was right there waiting.

He was so sweet." She sighs, stands up. "I cannot tell you, Elizabeth, what being near him means to me. And you made it possible. How do I thank you."

"There's no need," I say impatiently. "Sit down." We both do, on the corner of the bed. "Tell me what happened." I am concerned that perhaps I have made things go too far to control.

She is silent. "You have kissed?" I ask, in a low voice.

Lilith nods. She blushes. "And more."

"You made love?"

"No, not exactly," she responds. "Duke knows I am not ready – not yet. He promises I can take my time – whatever time I need. He will wait. He respects me," this said with such pride.

"I know he does, Lilith. He is that kind of a man – and he knows you are worthy of that respect."

"Oh, Elizabeth, we love each other. He is frantic over the arranged marriage in my future - says he will not let it happen. I am frantic too," and she starts to cry.

I let her weep for a minute, find the Kleenex, and as she revives, I question her further.

"How did you leave it? When do you see each other again?"

"Oh I don't know," she wails. "Willie was afraid that Ahmed might have seen us crossing the street. He was very nervous on our return here."

"Well, I think the next meeting should be in the Marais district, at Brit's house. It would be safer."

"Oh, yes." Lilith's discomfort stops. "Monsieur Brit's house! How generous of him."

I wonder how in blazes that transport across the city can be arranged. But arranged it will be. We are not resourceful for nothing.

"Look, don your burka. It's getting dark. Go find Willie and creep back into The Majestic. Will your parents be in their suite?"

"I don't think so. They were driving to Chartres this afternoon to see the Cathedral. I don't think they'll be back until later. They wanted me to go, but I said I was unwell."

"Hopefully you will return safely to your suite. If anyone of your group questions you…"

"Oh, I'll just say I was bored to death and wanted a little walk." Lilith kisses me. "I don't know how…"

"Hush, Lilith. It's my pleasure." I felt dumb saying that, but I meant it. She is gone.

I skip supper. The macaroons lie heavy in my stomach. I toss about in the bed, sleepless, worried, until a call from Brit gives me peace and hope and happiness. We plan to meet tomorrow night, and I tell him of the meeting of Duke and Lilith and how fraught with danger it seemed. The offer of his house, he repeats to me and assures me, transport will be arranged in his car, the old Peugeot.

"What would I do without you," I exclaim.

"That's not going to happen," he replies, and bids me a loving goodnight.

It is suddenly Monday morning. And it is later than usual when I go downstairs to breakfast. Willie is there at the desk. Jean-Luc is back in his office, with door open. He waves 'hello' from his chair, phone plastered to one ear, as I pass.

Willie beckons me over. The salon is full of hotel clients. Willie, in a low voice, tells me of his anxiety about Ahmed. "I'm quite sure he noticed me and the Arab Miss, just as we rounded the corner on our way back to the Hotel Marcel, last evening. She had her hair loose and looked more like herself."

"Oh God." This is disturbing. "Next time, we will take her to Brit's house in the Marais."

"If there be a next time," Willie says dolefully.

"Willie, there has to be."

"Them Arabs – those people are something to be reckoned with. They could take me job."

"I know, but Jean-Luc would make you permanent here, I know."

Willie gives a little smile and sigh of relief.

I proceed in to a breakfast repast that I have come to relish – the hot *café au lait, croissant,* fresh from the bakery, and all the delicious accompaniments. Believe me, I'm hungry. Supper last night was non-existent, so I eat slowly, savoring each morsel, each sip, as the touristy group leaves the salon in pairs and threesomes to attack the charms of Paris on a sunny day in May.

And tonight, I will be with MY love, the two of us living *la vie en rose* in elderly bliss and plotting our next move in bringing the young *amants* together.

Quelle vie!

CHAPTER FOURTEEN

Troubles Afoot

AS I COME downstairs on Tuesday morning, in the clinking, old *ascenseur*, I hear Jean-Luc on the phone in the office. His voice is loud, upset. The door is ajar. He waves me into the room, disconnects the phone line, rises and closes the door behind me as I enter.

"I can't believe that woman!" He is spluttering.

"Not Isabella?"

He looks at me in surprise. "Of course not. *Non, non,* that Croix woman. Do you know what she had the gall to say just now?" He returns to the chair behind his desk. "'I hate country living.'" Jean-Luc is mimicking her tone of voice. "'There's no one here interesting…nothing exciting. I miss Paris.' Then she has the audacity to tell me she must buy back the apartment! Can you imagine?"

"No!"

"Yes, yes. She will give me an extra 100,000 euros to rebuy MY apartment." Jean-Luc is genuinely upset.

"You're kidding."

"I wish I were. Of course, I told her absolutely not, but I know her. She will be after me, wearing me down, nagging at me. I wish we hadn't asked her to come to the wedding reception on Friday. If I had known…"

"Now calm down, Jean-Luc. There is no way she can make you sell it back to her."

He is mumbling to himself. "She can be such *une souffrance* - you know, a pain."

"I know, but she really can't DO anything about your living arrangements, now can she?" To change the subject, I tell him that I have seen Pierre Frontenac on the street and how thin he has become, a shadow of his former self.

Jean-Luc frowns. "Poor man. I know he is distressed over that *docteur* –you know, that friend of yours…"

"No friend of mine!"

"Well, your – how you say – acquaintance?"

"I guess you can call him that," I say with a *moue* of disapproval. "You know about him and Elise?"

"The whole street knows!"

"*Mon Dieu.* Is Sylvie LaGrange aware of the 'goings-on' too?"

"But of course. *Bien sûr.* René is watching her because the woman is violent. Sylvie considers *le bon docteur* her private property. Elise Frontenac has become her problem and *Sylvie est furieux!* Who knows what she might do?"

With this interchange, I leave my host and proceed to breakfast and dream of my evening with Brit, only last night, where we made plans for him to come to my home on Long Island the coming July and spend a full two months with me next to the ocean, living, swimming, cooking, and, of course, painting. What a joy to look forward to.

We also planned the rescue of Lilith, should she wish to meet Duke at Brit's house. (Of course she will!) He would collect her in the Peugeot and whisk her across the Seine to his digs near La Place des Vosges. Duke could make his way by himself. Having them both in the car 'might be risky,' Brit said. "Someone might see the two together and there'd be all hell to pay."

Brit is right, of course.

To me, he's almost always right!

CHAPTER FIFTEEN

Lilith's Intended

I RETURN THIS Tuesday evening, a little after 10:00 from a dinner date with Sasha, who now that Lilith is back in Paris, is trying to make contact with her. We had eaten a simple bowl of spaghetti with clam sauce, accompanied by a bottle of *Chianti*, followed by a rich *panne cotta* with berries.

"Who better than you, Elizabeth, to persuade her?" Sasha had said. "I want that girl for more pictures. She's the kind you can't get out of your mind...worth her weight in gold."

I grimace at this.

"Ah, come on. A man has to make a living."

"At someone else's expense?"

"Ah, Elizabeth."

"Look Sasha, I'll speak to her, but I doubt that modeling is uppermost in her thoughts right now."

"I'd be grateful," is his response.

Back at the Hotel Marcel, Willie has just arrived from his duties at The Majestic, and lets me in as I ring the bell. The lobby is empty, the whole first floor mutely lighted and silent.

"Madame Elizabeth, have you a minute? I have had quite a day."

"Of course, Willie."

"You're not too tired?"

I laugh. "Not at all."

"Well, it's like this," he says from behind the check-in desk, as I lean against it, both elbows crooked and hands holding my face. "I'm all yours," I say with a smile.

"I am in the suite – Monsoor Hamad al-Boudi's suite – you know, this afternoon, serving appetizers and tea to the sheikh and his wife, as I was ordered to do. You know, room service. The sheikh asked me to stay as they had a visitor coming and soon enough, that bloke Saud al-Alami arrives."

"What'd he look like, Willie?" I ask eagerly.

"Ya know, like a gentleman from the Middle East in robes and that white cloth around his head. He didn't look like much to me, kind of skinny with a wee moustache above his lip."

"How old?"

"Mid-age, I would guess," Willie says.

"Was Lilith there?"

"Not yet. The Saud fellow, he took some tea. He ate a little toast with *paté* on it and some anchovies. They was all babbling in Araby – not the Missus – blimey, she's some sour puss – but the two men. Couldn't understand a word between the two, a course, but I gotta sense they were – you know – kind of pleased with each other, that Saud had sent some sort of present because Monsoor Hamad kept kinda bowing his head in thanks, ya know what I mean?"

"I think so," I say. There is a pause. "And?" I am beyond curious.

"Well, after a few minutes, she came in."

"Lilith."

"Oh, my, Missus Elizabeth. She was beautiful! Blimey, I never seen prettier. She had on a long gold and red dress, and her hair it was in a kinda snood — you know, that net thing a woman wears to hold back her hair, but of course, it was made of gold too." Willie gestures with his hands behind his head.

"I'll just bet that dress and head covering were a gift from Saud." I'm positive it was a design of Rashid's, the new couturier from The Emirates Saud is backing, of whom Isabella told me about. "I'm sure of it. Rashid!" I blurt out, "the new designer of 'modest Muslim' clothes."

"Rashid? Who is Rashid?" Willie says, confused.

"I'm sorry, Willie. I'm just talking to myself, but tell me, how did Hamad and Saud react when they saw her? And her mother too?"

"React?"

"You know. Did they exclaim over her?"

"Oh, my yes! Particularly Saud. I guessed the fellow had never met her before, and he was mighty pleased with that vision of a girl before him, oh yes, mighty pleased, like he was lickin' his chops."

"Oh, God," I say. "Poor little Lilith." After a moment, I ask Willie, "How did Lilith look? I mean was she smiling — or anything?" I feel quite desperate for her.

"Smiling!" Willie explodes. "Not on you're your life, Missus. She looked about to cry, but she didn't. No tears showed, but I could tell she was very sad. And scairt, too. Really scairt. She looked like she thought she was about to be eaten by lions, that poor little Miss Lilith."

Eaten by lions. Oh, yes. Poor little Miss Lilith.

Not if I can help it.

CHAPTER SIXTEEN

If Looks Could Kill

DUKE RESERVES A long table at *Le Club* for his father's after-dinner birthday party. It seats eight: Pierre and Elise, Jean-Luc and Isabella, and Brit and me. There is a chair next to his father for Duke between sets, and an empty one on the other side of him. (For the absent Lilith?)

He places votive candles in a parade down the center of the white cloth, draping over the tabletop, with ice buckets at each end holding bottles of champagne. At the seat at the far end (his father's,) there is a box wrapped in silver paper, slim, long, in the shape of the tie Duke has bought as birthday present, inside.

All is prepared, this Wednesday evening, including the musicians who have practiced 'Happy Birthday.' A chocolate cake from *Le Nôtre*, with candles – six in all because Pierre is turning 60 – is ready to be lit, hidden behind the bar.

However, Duke is troubled. His thoughts of 'interruptus' of Dr. Paxière and Elise torments him, makes him tender towards his father, and deeply uncertain about his father's wife.

"Of course I didn't tell him," Duke says to me, over breakfast at Hotel Marcel, that same Wednesday morning. "It would kill him." He pauses, thoughtful." I guess I have to forgive her. After all, my father – his history with my mother…" he continues. "Do you think this is Elise's way of pay-back?"

"No," I say. "I really believe Paxière is a serial adulterer, addicted to conquest, and with a very weak ego that needs constant reassurance. But I guess, for some, he is hard to resist." (Not to me, I think, smugly.)

This conversation earlier in the day stays with me. I am curious as to how this evening will unfold. And it begins in an ordinary enough way. However, I observe the faces of Elise and Pierre, hers rosier, softer, less sharp than I've ever seen her: the other, Pierre's, grayer, thinner, older. They barely speak to one another.

We are gathered here, at the table, in the center section of *Le Club*. We collectively have brought a large bouquet of mixed blossoms in a low crystal bowl, which is now the centerpiece. Other customers look about at us, curiously, but spirits are high, festive. The music plays a gay rendition of 'After You've Gone,' Duke up there on stage, on bass. People are clapping along, eager to join in the celebration.

As the set finishes, Duke steps down and takes his seat next to his father. He signals the bar to bring the cake, the musicians to play the birthday song, and the waiters to pour champagne. All goes off without a hitch, Pierre smiling broadly for the first time, patting his son's hand, and truly touched when Elise hands him a small black box and leans over to kiss him on the cheek.

He cuts the cake, which is distributed about the table on dessert plates by the waiters. He opens first, Duke's tie, which is a conservative gray and blue plaid, very handsome, over which Pierre exclaims. He lifts the lid off the box from his wife and holds up a simple, silver tiepin. Obviously pleased, he looks to both wife and son, and I see a glint of moisture in his eyes. It is a sweet moment, soon to be interrupted by the appearance, coming forth from the shadowy club towards the table, the figure of Guillaume Paxière!

Mon Dieu.

We are all frozen, silent, as Guillaume approaches the table. He goes directly to Elise, who looks caught in amber, picks up her hand from the table, and kisses it. Then, turning to Pierre, he gives salutations to him for his birthday and wishes him a happy coming year, this said with a sardonic bow. He turns and leaves.

Duke is on his feet, his hands in fists. Pierre looks humiliated, as Elise tries to blushingly hide her pleasure at the sight of her lover, and frankly, the mood at the table is dead. Dead as a doornail. I know that's a trite way to put it, but there is no other.

As I look across the room, following the back of the good *docteur*, I see at a corner table near the door, the flushed face of Sylvie LaGrange. She awaits her returning lover with an obvious ambivalence, chewing her lip anxiously, yet glaring across the sea of people at Elise.

Elise has seen Sylvie too. The look between these two ladies is palpable, a look of pure hatred and disgust. I believe they both know what is going on with Paxière's treachery, that he has betrayed each woman in his own special way, and that he is thoroughly enjoying the womanly war he has instigated.

Quel bâtard!

Duke is called to the stage to resume playing which he does reluctantly. He is furious at the interruption of the goodwill created at his father's birthday celebration. All has been turned to ashes.

At the table, conversation is desultory. Brit tries to draw Pierre into a discussion of art-world politics, which Pierre is known to follow. But all of us, and I mean ALL, are secretly eying the couple over by the door. Sylvie has her arm through the arm of Paxière, her hand clasping his, on top of the small table. Her eyes, when not fixed on his lips, which she occasionally leans across to kiss, are directed at Elise with a triumphal expression that is, frankly, disgusting.

At one point, we see her caress his leg and kiss him more passionately, at which I can hear Elise let out an extreme sigh as she closes her eyes. This is not lost on Pierre.

Brit tries to save the day (for some of us) by lifting a glass to Pierre who receives the toast gracefully enough until he notices Elise is about to cry. She has always been prone to tears when feeling helpless. He realizes they must leave. He gathers his presents and stands, at which point I see Sylvie, literally drag Guillaume to his feet and rush toward us as we prepare to quit *Le Club*.

Clutching the doctor, pressing his arm against her breast, she says to Pierre, "Ah, Monsieur Frontenac, I did not have the chance to wish you a most happy birthday," (glancing at Elise.) "My good friend, Dr. Guillaume Paxière, came over here before I was able to, but I wish God speed to you now."

Pierre, nonplussed, merely gives a little bow of acknowledgement.

"We're off," Sylvie is saying as we try to walk past and out, Pierre carrying the bowl of flowers, our gift of the evening. "Come along, *mon amour*," Sylvie whispers to Paxière, loud enough for all to hear. "Take me home."

And the bastard is enjoying the whole thing!

CHAPTER SEVENTEEN

High Risk

I HAVE A headache after last night over the performance of that LaGrange harridan and her complicit lover, on this Thursday morning. It is not only my concern for Pierre Frontenac, causing me pain, but there is a very real dread of how to save Lilith from the proverbial fate worse than death.

My anxiety is heightened when I see René Poignal in the lobby. He is speaking to Jean-Luc quietly, over the check-in desk counter, behind which my hotelier sits. There are people, noisily eating breakfast in the salon.

I stop to speak to my two friends up front. "What a night," I exclaim to Jean-Luc, wiping my brow.

"You can say that again," he says solemnly.

"Am I missing something?" René questions, and I briefly tell him of the birthday party broken in half by the appearance of Sylvie and the *docteur*, the dismay of Elise, and the true pain of Pierre Frontenac. "It was a disaster."

"Hmm. Sounds like," René comments. "Those two women…" He shakes his head. "I see a bad end to this, but what is one to do? How to stop the inevitable?" He looks about him. "There is something more that is even more troubling. I am worried about Ahmed, you know, the bodyguard next door – with the al-Boudi group. I have noticed him stalking people at Hotel Marcel – seen him skulking around, very suspicious."

"Ah, not again!" Jean-Luc says, quite loudly, striking his forehead.

"Who do you think he's watching," I ask, knowing full well the answer.

"Not sure…but I do know he keeps his eyes on Willie Blakely. I bet he knows you've got him working here on his off hours from The Majestic."

"Oh God," I exclaim.

"Aha!" the good detective says. "You know something, Madame Elizabeth?"

"Not much," I mumble. "It's just that …Willie is such a nice fellow. I hope Ahmed doesn't get him fired."

And it is at just this moment that we see Willie enter the lobby. He looks distressed, a bit disheveled, shocked.

Jean-Luc rises. He goes to the kitchen at the back of the salon and summons Brigitte to replace him at the front desk.

"Come back to my room," he says to the three of us, and René, Willie and I dutifully follow him to the tiny, cluttered space he calls his office.

Sitting behind his desk, as we stand in a row like proper children, he asks Willie, "What's up?"

"I be fired," Willie blurts out with a choke in his voice. "Fired!"

"Ah, Willie. I am sorry – but you know you can have a permanent job with me," Jean-Luc says –"if you want it."

"Oh, Sir, I be most grateful. I do thank you. Of course, I want it. 'T'is the happiest place to work I ever seen. And the people." He looks at René. He looks at me. "They be…" and he chokes up, bowing his head.

"Come, now," René chimes in. "Willie, do they know you're over here now?"

"I giss so. That be one of the reasons I be fired. I be disloyal – although why having a second job is disloyal, beats me." He snivels. "I have to go back to me locker and get me stuff, and then it's all over, Majestic, and good riddance." He squares his shoulders.

René turns to leave. "I got duties to perform," he says, and to Willie, kindly," All the best of luck Willie. With Jean-Luc here, you landed on your feet. You'll see. Things will get better."

"Thank you," Willie says. For the first time he smiles.

With René gone, I feel free to ask Willie if, when he is collecting his things, he might collect Lilith too!

It is a bold move, but without him at The Majestic, we have no way of reaching her. She will be lost to us and to Duke, and married to Saud and a miserable life.

"She knows what's in store for her, Willie, if we can't help her escape. Do you think you could possibly at least try to call her – and tell her to come down with no possessions – nothing at all - in her burka…"

"And with her passport," Jean-Luc interjects.

At first Willie looks askance, but his face relaxes. "That poor little thing."

He pauses. "I can tell her about the passport, I giss I can try. It depends – on so many…but yes, I'll try and with a little bit o' luck…it might work."

"Bring her here to me, Okay Willie? I know she will thank you. I know she is desperate, poor child. In despair."

"She'd rather die than marry that Saud fella," Willie says firmly. "I'll try."

When he is off on his mission, I turn to Jean-Luc. "Passport?" I question.

"You don't think she can stay here in Paris with that mob next door chasing her. Besides, I'll bet Duke wants to take her to America."

"But her passport – the picture – the authorities might recognize her if she tries to leave the country."

"Sasha can take care of that. He's an all-time fixer," Jean-Luc says with a grin. "And he can do it fast."

"Now all we have to do is wait."

"You can stay here in the office, if you like," Jean-Luc says. "I'd better get up front."

And I do stay. I sit behind his desk. It seems interminable, the waiting. I am beyond tapping my fingers. I get up and pace. I inspect a glass case where Jean-Luc has a collection of china bellboys, an odd assortment that he cherishes. I sit again, and then in seconds it seems, Lilith, in burka, bursts into the room, Willie not far behind.

She is crying. She clutches me. "I know this is the end. I can never go back. But I would rather die than marry that man. I have to escape."

"I know, I know," I say. "Sit a minute. Calm down a bit. I'm going to call Brit right now. He will bring his car for us and take us to his house on the other side of the river."

I do call. He is on his way. Jean-Luc brings hot tea for Lilith, who sits on the side chair. Brit appears. Lilith and I climb into the Peugeot unnoticed by those next door. She sheds her burka in the back seat, as I call Duke on his cell phone and give him Brit's address.

We're there on the rue de Chance, safe in Brit's small townhouse. He has already placed an inflatable mattress on the floor of the salon downstairs (for himself.) Lilith will have the upstairs workroom, with bed in one corner and bathroom adjacent, for the time being. My love is indeed a thoughtful man.

From the time Willie first appeared in the lobby of Hotel Marcel this morning, until now, at #2 Bis, rue de Chance in the Marais district, with our escapee rescued and in our care, the whole miraculous adventure has taken less than three hours!

To me, it has been an eternity.

CHAPTER EIGHTEEN

Safe Haven

EVEN THOUGH IT is barely noon, on this Thursday morning, Lilith is lying down on Brit's bed on the second floor of his townhouse. He has placed a sheet over the bedclothes, a coverlet in pink near her feet, and given her a fresh pillow for under her head. I sit beside her in a chair, drawn close.

She is silent, then suddenly says, "It's decided. I can never go home again." Then, "But there is no home for me there anyway." Her tone is wistful.

"Ah, Lilith," I say softly.

"I can't believe my mother. She was worse than father, about the marriage, insisting that I will adjust, that I will come to love this man – and if I don't, well, that is life, she says, the way things are ordered. She calls me ungrateful." Lilith sighs. "I guess maybe I am."

"Oh no, Lilith."

"I don't want to shame my family. I do not want to insult Saud al-Alami by refusing him. But the thought of him touching me – with his little tiny fingers and the wispy hair above his lip!" She shudders. "Besides, as you know, Elizabeth, I love someone else." With that, Lilith rolls on her side, her hand under her cheek. "You know I love Duke."

"I know," I say. "Your mother doesn't know about him?"

"Oh no!"

"Just as well. But I am sorry your mother couldn't understand your feelings about Saud, that you really couldn't stand him."

"My mother is so determined, and she can be cold. She bows down totally to my father. Even with his other women, she looks away and keeps an icy control." Lilith sits up, throws her arms about me. "Oh, Elizabeth, I would become the same if I married that man. I would turn to ice too – even with my babies."

"It's not going to happen. You won't have to marry Saud. Quite honestly, Lilith, by running away with us so abruptly, you have to realize -"

"I can never go home again. I mean it. There is no place for me there in Qatar, in my family, and no place here in Paris with Saud. I know it. I accept it."

"How? How can you accept it?" I question, truly to test her decisiveness.

She looks at me, and in the most mature voice she has ever used, she says, "Because I must."

I smile at her.

"And besides," she says beaming suddenly. "There is Duke. There is a future, and it is mine."

As she says this, pounding eagerly up the stairs, Duke flings himself into the upstairs room. He goes directly to Lilith. He says nothing but cradles her in his arms. Brit had apparently called him and told him that Lilith was at his house, unknown to her family and truly alone in the world. Duke's response was immediate. He grabbed the nearest taxi.

I look away from the two of them, hearing nothing but sweet murmurs. Finally, I say, "Look, you two. Lilith is going to need some clothes. I'm going over to *Printemps*, you know, the department store on the Right Bank, and get something for her to wear," and with a big smile, I leave them alone and I'm off on my errand.

Returning later in the afternoon, with packages in hand, I present Lilith with a variety of new garments: blue jeans, a couple of tee shirts, one white, one navy blue, a light-weight cardigan in dark gray, a variety of underwear, even a small backpack to put them in. I also had purchased a boy's visored cap in black linen and a pair of dark glasses.

Lilith inspects these items, exclaiming over and over, "I have never worn blue jeans. I have never had a cap like this," and she puts it on her hair at a rakish angle. Obviously, she is thrilled.

Duke is looking on with delight.

Brit calls from downstairs. "I have dinner for you down here. Come and get it."

The three of us descend the stairs to the most intoxicating aroma of Chinese cookery. Brit, not known for his domestic talents, does have one specialty: stir fry! He had gone out and bought a supply of lean-cut beef, broccoli, rice, soy sauce, ginger, garlic, sesame oil, and as we come into the salon, I see him at his wok in the tiny kitchen, busily sautéing the delicious combination.

"Elizabeth, there's *Sauvignon Blanc* in the ice box. The glasses are on the shelf." He turns to me with a flourish. "I even bought chopsticks!"

The four of us sit down, Duke on a stool by the fireplace, and devour a truly delicious Chinese dinner!

As we demolish the savory beef, Duke speaks of taking Lilith to America. "We talked about it upstairs," he says, looking across at her lovingly. "I want to bring her to Chicago, to my sister's house where she lives with a very nice fellow, a white man, who has a car dealership."

"Do you think this is the best idea?" asks Brit.

"She certainly can't stay here," I interject.

"Of course not," Duke says. "Her father must know by now she is missing. They'll be out looking for her."

"I'm sorry to be such a bother," Lilith says "I'm getting you all into trouble."

"Come, now, Lilith," Brit says kindly. "You are worth it."

"Did you bring your passport with you?" I ask.

"Yes. I have it upstairs. Mother keeps them all in a leather case in her room. When she was out, I found mine. It was at the bottom so she might not notice it is gone."

"No but they will certainly notice your absence, your lack of being around," Brit says sardonically.

"I think we better change your look, and the new clothes won't do it," I say. "I'm afraid, if you got to the airport with the same passport picture, well, you might be stopped, particularly if your father has informed the authorities there to look out for you."

"Oh lord. He would do that," she says, blanching.

"Well, we'll just have to disguise you, some way, and Sasha can take a new passport picture. He knows how to do these things. He's been all over the world and is very speedy. By the way, does your father know anything of Duke?" I continue.

"No. No. He doesn't. Mother too. She doesn't know."

"Well," says Brit. "That will surely change."

Duke rises to his feet, looks at his watch. "God, I have to go to work."

He turns to Lilith, leans down to her. "I plan to tell them I'm leaving tonight. If you're sure, Lilith, if you're sure you want to come away with me."

She nods her head slowly. "Absolutely," and she lifts her face up to his. They exchange a long look.

"I must go too," I say, breaking the spell. "Could you drop me off at the hotel, Duke? It's a bit out of your way, but…"

"Of course," he says.

With kisses all around, we leave. Tomorrow is the wedding, of Jean-Luc and Isabella. Brit and I will be there at the *Mairie* and at the reception afterward, to which Duke will come later. Not Lilith, of course. That would be an immensely stupid risk.

CHAPTER NINETEEN

A Wedding to Remember

BRIT AND I meet at the *Mairie*. It is very close to the Hotel Marcel, on the rue de Grenelle. It is a large building set back off the street, with a clock tower.

Brit and I go to the *État Civil* desk in the lobby and are directed to a room on the second floor where the marriage service will be held. I am in my blue dress from Yves St. Laurent and carry a corsage of *fleur de lis*, the flower of 'luck.' Brit carries a small abstract painting of The Eiffel Tower he has done, from the perspective of underneath the huge structure, looking up. It is a beautiful work and our wedding present to the Marcels. We arrive 15 minutes before the great event, on this Friday afternoon, about 3:45, all excited.

Brit and I do not need such a service. However, it is wonderful to see the younger pair, Jean-Luc and Isabella, making the move, building a conjoined life together. Perhaps children will come along. Isabella is surely young enough, and Jean-Luc, already a father of two teen-age boys, is perhaps eager for a little baby girl (or boy), as long as it is Isabella's.

The two are already there. She wears an exquisite, short dress in white, with long lace sleeves. The body of the dress has tiny rose-colored flowers and pale green ivy sprinkled about and the affect is ravishing, with her face glowing, the shiny dark hair pulled back in a chignon. She carries a bouquet of pink and red roses.

Sasha is there for Jean-Luc, as witness. The magistrate enters the room, an elderly man in a black robe, with a chain of office about his neck. We all stand. The service is brief, mumbled in French, completed with a kiss between the newly married. After signing some papers, the five of us descend to the street and walk back up the avenue to Jean-Luc's new apartment on this radiant afternoon. We compose a wedding party for all the world to see.

Willie Blakely is at the door of Jean-Luc's apartment, with a tray carrying flutes of champagne for each of us.

"I wouldn't miss yer nuptial party, now would I," Willie exclaims. "Congratulations, Missus Isabella."

"Why, thank you, Willie," she says, taking a flute in one hand, handing Jean-Luc his champagne with the other. With that, Willie places the tray down and brings forth from the oven, delectable *croutons* topped with crabmeat in a bubbling *béchamel* sauce.

"You made these, Willie?" I proclaim. "They are fabulous."

"Yes, Missus Elizabeth. I'm a jack of all trades," he says, obviously pleased.

"Willie, you are a marvel," Jean-Luc says, joining us.

"Ya know how grateful I am, Monsoor Marcel, ya know, for me job."

Willie retreats, bringing forth this time, a cheese board set with grapes and crackers, just as the doorbell rings. He moves to the front door, and who enters but Ray Guild and the Croix couple, Louise resplendent in a bright flowered dress and her customary purplish lipstick. Ray carries a magnum of champagne, properly chilled, and Edouard Croix brings a large bouquet of white lilies from their home garden near the Fontainebleau Forest. Louise has provided a lined wicker basket to hold them.

"How beautiful!" Isabella exclaims, and places the basket on a low table by the window. At this point, Brit presents his painting to Jean-Luc and his bride, saying, "From both Elizabeth and me. Long life and happiness," and he raises his glass in a toast.

The painting is extraordinary and both bride and groom are visibly thrilled by this gift. Isabella takes the canvas to the wall next to the window. "We shall hang it just here! We cannot actually see The Eiffel Tower from this window, but now we will have this special vision of it inside our home."

Louise Croix is looking at the picture critically. "It looks kind of upside down," she says.

"It is painted from the perspective of underneath the structure," Brit says in an amazingly patient tone.

"Oh, I see," Louise says, and turns away.

Sasha has been busily taking pictures of the newlyweds and of the various people in the room, while munching on grapes and cheese and the crabmeat croutons. "My present is going to be a book of photos from this great moment. I got some really good shots at the *Mairie*, even of the old judge."

"Sasha, I need a favor," I say, in a low voice, moving close to him. "Tomorrow afternoon, would you be free to come to Brit's Marais town house and take a special passport photo for me?"

"Why, I think so. Sure. In the afternoon? Maybe around 5:00 o'clock?"

"Perfect," I say, as I give him a note with Brit's address. "We'll give you a drink."

"I would expect no less," he says with a grin.

The Frontenac's have joined the party, their demeanor subdued. Elise is extremely pale, and her husband, Pierre, rather distant, but they congratulate Jean-Luc and Isabella with genuine warmth.

I hear Louise Croix say to Jean-Luc, as she and Edouard prepare to leave, "You haven't forgotten my offer to reclaim this apartment, have you?"

"It hasn't left my thoughts for a moment, dear Louise. But the answer is still no." Jean-Luc tries to make light of the situation. "You must begin to enjoy the country life. It is May. The beautiful lilies are blooming," he says, pointing to their basket of flowers on the table by the window. "It is the good life of the country squire and squiress."

"Bah," Louise responds. "Squiress indeed! It is a pitiable life, so boring. I need to be in Paris, where there are people to amuse one."

"And your gossip, to spread," I say pointedly.

She glares at me. "I am not giving up," she insists, turning to Jean-Luc. I will have my apartment back!"

"Pas de chance, Louise. *Pas de chance."* Jean-Luc is adamant.

"We'll see," she says, and grabbing Edouard's arm, the two leave for the country life.

René Poignal appears. "I have only a few minutes, Jean-Luc, but I have to bring you my best wishes to both of you," and he shyly kisses Isabella on the cheek.

"I appreciate your coming," Jean-Luc says. "We have become good friends, over the past couple of years. I am glad. It's nice to be on the good side of the law," and the two men laugh. René accepts a flute of champagne happily and raises his glass. "To one and all on this great occasion," he says, downs the wine in one gulp, and with the words, "I should not drink on duty," is off to the street he patrols and loves.

The last to arrive is Duke Davis. He comes into the party with a smile, and after approaching the bridal couple by the window, congratulating them effusively, he makes a bee-line for me. "Elizabeth. I am off to *Le Club* in a moment. This is my last night. I told them yesterday that I was leaving and it was for family reasons, that's why the short notice."

"How did they take it?"

"They were really nice. They said I would always have a job if I come back, and they hoped I would, once I took care of my family situation. The owner said they've never had a bass player who could also play jazz violin." As he says this, Pierre and Elise Frontenac come over to the two of us. Duke touches his father's shoulder. He looks into his eyes. There is a real connection. "I have to tell you, sir, that I am leaving for America in a few days."

"No," Pierre says, looking genuinely upset.

"I must, sir," Duke says respectfully. "I plan to go to Chicago – to my sister's. It's a critical situation. I must be there for her. Please understand."

"I guess I must, son."

"You are a good brother," Elise says. "But you will come back?"

"Oh, I hope so. I expect to," Duke says, grateful for her intrusion.

"Well, if and when you do," she continues, "You will always have a home with us."

Pierre looks at her with an expression of surprise and, of a sudden, affection. He is obviously touched.

Brit and I begin to take our leave, with many pleasantries and exclamations of good will. "The honeymoon?" Brit questions.

"We'll be around for the next weeks," Jean says, "but in June, we're going to a little town in the Pyrenees, a place near where Isabella was born, for a few days. Then, we go to Sitges on the Costa Brava of Spain where she grew up." His young wife is beaming.

"Sounds wonderful," I say. "You both deserve a honeymoon out of Paris and hotelier responsibilities."

"Willie will come in handy, for sure. *Bien sûr.*"

"How will I be handy?" Willie says, coming up to our little group.

"Doing hotel duties, my man, while Isabella and I are on our honeymoon trip." Willie looks extremely pleased at being so necessary to his boss.

I pull Willie aside for a second. "Could you come to Brit's house tomorrow in the morning. We have to do something about Lilith's look, maybe cut her hair or something. Do you have any ideas?"

"I think so. I could pick up some blonde dye for her hair," and then shyly, "you know, I was a barber in the beginning of my career."

"You were?" I say, quite astonished.

"Yes. My first job."

"Then come tomorrow. And don't forget. Bring scissors!"

CHAPTER TWENTY

Blonde

AS I COME up the stairs in Brit's townhouse on Saturday morning, I can hear through the bathroom door, first, the sounds of clipping scissors, and the murmur of protest. "Aye, don't cry Missy. It'll grow back. Don't you worry none. This is just for now."

Willie is speaking non-stop to soothe the girl under the scissors. "Ya know, my very first job was barbering. I started in Liverpool as a young-un, at a little place belonging to my uncle. Oh, I had to learn the trade all right, but after a couple years, I took up waitering, first in Liverpool, me hometown, and then, later, I went up to London. Pay was better. I worked my way into Claridge's dining room! Now, that's a proud place. Been waitering ever since. But I ain't forgotten my original trade. No, Ma'am."

"There," he says. I here the sound of water splashing, and then, her laughter like tinkling glass. Then silence.

"It's cold," I hear her say a bit later.

"That's the chemicals, Miss. In a minute I'll put on the toner, than wash you clean, and you will come out a blonde lady, not brassy blonde, but kind of ashy color, and Missy, you'll be beautiful."

"Thank you, Willie," I hear her say in a sweet voice. "I do thank you."

And she does appear beautiful. Swathed in white towels, her hair still slightly wet, the face glowing, Lilith comes from the bathroom, barefoot. Her light colored hair reaches her chin line. She looks a modern girl, and an exceptionally pretty one at that.

"Willie, you are a master," I say, ebulliently. "What a job!"

He beams at the praise. "I ain't forgotten," he says, very pleased with himself. "She does look mighty good, now, doesn't she, and so different."

"Exactly. It's just what we need for her passport picture."

"I wonder what Duke will think," she suddenly says, alarm spreading across her face.

"He'll still love you, I guarantee," I say with a smile. "Now, put on some of the clothes I brought you."

Lilith disappears back into the bathroom with a big grin, carrying a sack of the *Printemps* clothing I had bought.

She emerges tentatively, just as Duke comes up the stairs. He stops cold in his tracks. His jaw drops as he looks at his girl, in her denim jeans, dark blue tee shirt, and soft, light hair. "Lilith!" bursts out of him, "Lilith," and he suddenly throws his head back and laughs. "You look… you look so…"

"Different?" she says.

"You could say so," he says, going to her and taking her in his arms. "Different, yes, but oh so beautiful."

Willie and I go downstairs and leave the two to talk and plan their next moves.

Brit, in his kitchen, comes forth with a cup each of plain, black American coffee which Willie and I both accept with gratitude. I surely need it, and so does Willie after his successful labors in the room above.

"I have something to show you," Brit says. He goes to the corner near the fireplace and brings forth his sketch pad which he opens. On the page is an ethereal drawing of Lilith in charcoal, a 'before' Lilith with long, curling black hair. The title at the top? *Jeune Fille Dormante*, 'Young Girl Sleeping.' "I drew this last night when I went up to check on her. She was sound asleep and looked so young and vulnerable, I couldn't help myself. I want to give it to them. Do you think I should?"

"Oh, yes. Yes. In the first place, it is so lovely and it's her, the way she was and will be again. I think both she and Duke will love it."

Brit smiles, satisfied. He calls upstairs, "Hey you two lovebirds. How about some lunch?" and the two young people come down stairs to a picnic of sorts that Brit is laying out; some slices of cold ham, tomatoes and cucumbers in a *vinaigrette*, a *baguette*, a variety of cheeses, and some pears and plums.

All of us dig in happily, as Brit rounds out the meal with glasses of *Merlot*.

"I'd best get back to the hotel," Willie remarks, getting to his feet. "This has been a really nice repast, Monsoor Brit, and I thank ye, but I best be off."

He nods to our little group. "You look jest fine, Missy, if I do say so meself."

"I am just fine," Lilith says, going to him and kissing him on the cheek. "Thank you for making me so different, Willie."

"Oh, you don't be different, Missy. I hope not. Jest a little bit yellower."

We all laugh, and Willie leaves amidst a round of thanks calling after him.

As we continue to enjoy the picnic in Brit's salon, and finally start the clean up, I ask Duke how his father feels about him returning to the States.

"He was a bit surprised when I told him, but he understands. I said it was about my sister, that she needed me in Chicago. Family business," he says, smiling at Lilith. He can't take his eyes off her new look.

"I'm glad," I say. I quite like Pierre. And Elise? Did she have any reaction?"

"She surprised me," Duke says. "Her first response was that I would always have a home with them. She – honestly – was very sweet."

"I hope the two are all right," I say. "That doctor business. It must bother Pierre a lot."

"I'm sure it does. I think he feels he has to put up with the 'flirtation?'" – Duke looks at Lilith – "because of his own terrific guilt about my mother. If he has confronted Elise, all she has to do is remind him of his own past. He was unfaithful first – even if it was more than 20 years ago."

I am suddenly embarrassed. "I didn't mean to bring up the past this way. It is really irrelevant. It's just that I don't know how he's able to stand what's going on right under his nose."

Duke looks over at Lilith. She seems perfectly calm about the conversation. "Lilith knows all about it. I tell her everything," he says gently. "We are totally honest together," at which, she nods.

"That's the way to be," I say, much relieved.

There is a tap at the front door. It is Sasha, camera in its case in hand. I find it hard to realize the afternoon is gone, but here is our photographer, ready and waiting. I see him look about, and his eyes come to rest on Lilith.

He actually does a double take!

"No! Is that you? Lilith? My God. You look like an American girl. It's fantastic."

"To me that is a big compliment," Lilith says with delight, getting to her feet. "Because I'm going to America. I will be a real American girl."

"When are you going to America?" Sasha says, taking a deep breath. "And, more important, why are you going to America?" He looks at all of us one by one.

"It's necessary, Sasha. Lilith has been pledged in marriage by her family to an older Arab man she cannot stand. Duke is taking her to live in Chicago with his sister and her family, at least for the moment, anything to get her out of town," I say quickly.

"Chicago! What's in Chicago?" Sasha is still in shock.

"Not only my sister," Duke says, "but a lot of good jazz and that means work for me."

"Here, let me get you a drink, Sasha," Brit says. "What'll it be?"

"Scotch, if you have it. I think I need one."

"Okay," I say. "Lilith needs a new passport picture."

"No problem," Sasha says, accepting the glass of several ounces of scotch, with ice cubes, that Brit hands him. "Come, my girl. Just sit over here on this stool."

Lilith complies happily. "I can't get over the way you look," Sasha exclaims. "It's uncanny. And you're just as beautiful blonde as you are with long black hair. I wish you weren't leaving the country. I could sure use you as a model."

"She has to," I say firmly.

"I know," says Sasha, adjusting his camera. He takes several shots. "That should do it. Now where's the passport?"

Duke runs upstairs and retrieves it, returning and handing it to Sasha.

"Just let me finish my drink," Sasha says, sitting on the nearest chair. "Then, I'll be away. I can get this back to you tomorrow," he says waving the passport in the air. "I have a guy who does this sort of thing all the time."

"Sounds illegal," Brit says with a smile.

"Oh, it is," Sasha says. "It is." Brit brings over the scotch bottle and adds a splash to Sasha's glass, which Sasha accepts with a merry smile.

At this point, Brit brings over to Lilith, where she sits next to Duke, the picture in charcoal he had drawn of her the previous night.

"You were sleeping. I couldn't resist," he says, handing the sheet to Lilith.

"It takes my breath away," says Duke.

"You can have it. It's for you, if you want it."

"Of course we want it," they both exclaim together.

"Just a minute," I interject. "I think it dangerous for you to take in your suitcase. Why don't I take it when I leave next week and send it to you in Chicago." Duke hands me the elegant, little drawing of Lilith sleeping, which I put in a folder that Brit gives me.

"Probably a good idea," says Sasha. "Don't want you to get stopped at the border!" He gets up to leave. "I hope I see you two again," he says to Lilith and Duke. "You make a sweet pair." Then to me, "I'll drop this off at the hotel tomorrow, okay?"

"Better than okay," I say. "And thanks, Sasha. I owe you."

"You bet," he says with a grin.

"Wait a second," I say. "Can you drop me off, Sasha?" Then, to Brit, I say, "I should get going too. I'm exhausted with all this drama."

"Of course. I think we are all wiped out."

"I'll be going too," says Duke. He hugs Lilith. "*À demain, chérie. Dormez bien.*" He gives her a long kiss. We look away. Then I kiss Brit and well, you know, finally, Duke, Sasha and I remove ourselves and return to the Left Bank and the sanity of the Hotel Marcel and the avenue where the three of us happen to operate.

Whew!

CHAPTER TWENTY-ONE

Insanity

I AM DOWNSTAIRS in the lobby early this Sunday morning. Willie is presiding at the front desk. His brow is furrowed. I can see he is deeply worried.

He speaks to me, telling me that another waiter at The Majestic, a man from Korea who he has befriended, came to him last night with a frightening tale of the wrath of Hamad al-Boudi.

"The sheikh is enraged. He has spoken to the police, has called the hospitals, looking for his daughter. Blimey, it has become a dire situation, Missus. He is threatening his bodyguard, Ahmed, with severe punishment if Lilith is not found – and right away! He blames the poor bloke for not protecting his daughter."

"What'll we do, Willie? What? More important, what CAN we do?"

His words are so disturbing.

"I can't say, Missus. But I'm scairt for meself too. First, Ahmed went to Nelson and got me fired. Ahmed fingered me, and now he is in trouble with the boss. Oh, he's been suspicious of me since the early days– always skulking around. I think he might have followed me when I went to Mr. Brit's house to cut Lilith's hair."

"No! Oh, God. You think he might know where she is now?"

"I can't say, Missus. But it's possible. And I'm sure Ahmed is desperate."

I go into the salon. There are two couples there finishing breakfast. Brigitte brings me my usual *café complet* but I can only drink the coffee black, and it is bitter.

I make a decision. Leaving the table, nodding to Willie as I pass, I go to my room on the fifth floor and put in a call to Sue.

She is immediately responsive on the phone when I tell her of the predicament.

"Bring the poor child here to me," is her first reaction. I am blown away by her empathy.

"Duke will be with her," I remark.

"Of course. I would expect no less. And you?"

"I think it would be too dangerous for me to be there – or even for Brit to drive them down to you. There is already suspicion about both of us. We may have been seen, even followed."

"Oh, good Lord," says Sue. "Well, who needs you?" she says, with a smile in her voice. "I can manage the two lovers. If they have papers, I can even have my driver take them to de Gaulle airport. But how will they get down here from Paris?"

"I think I can get Mounir to take them in his van. He always meets me at the airport, and I know he would love the money for a journey to your *château* in Montoire. Yes," I say, nodding to myself. "After I finish with you, I'll call him and get him over to the Marais house post-haste."

"Sounds like a plan," Sue says. As she is about to ring off, she asks, "Where in hell are they going? What is Duke going to do with his little Qatari lady?"

"He is planning to take her to Chicago."

"Chicago?" Sue explodes. "Why Chicago?"

"He has a sister there, married to a white man. I guess he feels it might be safe. I don't know exactly when this is all going to come down.

All I know is it will be soon. And look, when I know they are on their way to you, I'll call right away and let you know. Then, could you call de Gaulle and book their tickets, and make it coach, to O'Hare airport? I hate to ask…"

"Of course," is her immediate response.

"Naturally, Duke will reimburse you."

"No problem." Sue's voice is excited. "Oh goody! This is the most thrilling thing to happen since I became *châtelaine* of the *château*. An escape! And in the name of love!"

"In the name of love," I echo. And I hang up.

The phone rings right away. I pick up. "Sue?" But it is not she. It is Willie.

"Sasha is here," he says. "He has something for you."

"Would you ask him if he would come up?"

"He's on his way."

I wait anxiously the few minutes it takes for Sasha to appear at my door.

He hands me a small manila envelope. Inside is Lilith's new passport, as well as the old one. Her picture is astonishingly different from that taken in Qatar. In that she is solemn, with her dark hair in a chador, her shoulders burka-rized.

The new version, with shoulder length blonde hair, a dark blue tee shirt and gray cardigan, and a wide smile, is of a totally different girl. All the other information, the stamps, the visa markings, the pertinent information about Lilith is exactly the same.

"I'm impressed, Sasha. How did you do this?"

"Let's just say I've got friends in important places," he says with a huge grin. "Anything to help those two young people in love."

"You're a good man, Sasha."

"I know that," he says, and with a wave of his hand in goodbye, he leaves me and I hear his feet on the stairs.

And, miraculously, it comes about. I call Mounir. He is ready and eager. He will meet me downstairs in one hour so I can give him Lilith's passports, both old and new, and the address to Brit's house. He already knows the way to the *château* in Montoire. We have been there together more than once.

I then call Brit who alerts Duke, who is there cooking eggs for Lilith on Brit's range. The two are ready to leave. In fact, when I speak to Lilith on the phone, her excitement is palpable.

"Now, Lilith, my Sue, she's an old and trusted friend. I have known her for years. She is American but married a Marquis, who unfortunately passed away a few years ago. She knows all about you, and Duke."

"She lives in a *château?*"

"Oh, Sue is very real and down-to-earth. You will like her, I know, and she is only too glad to help you both. She's a romantic."

"Oh. I'm so glad she's romantic." I can tell from her voice that Lilith is smiling.

"Let me speak to Duke. And Lilith, remember, in the States, you can always come to me. I'll give Duke my address, and he will give me yours, and we will surely be together again, only in a different country."

"Oh, please. Make that happen, Elizabeth."

With him, I explain about Sue arranging ticketing for them and that her driver will chauffeur them to de Gaulle and that Sue is eager to be of help, in fact, that she is quite thrilled to be part of their adventure. We exchange address and phone information, and at the end of the call, Duke says, "I will never be able…" at which I interject, "Enough already. I will see you both again, Duke. I know it. I really don't want to lose you."

With a catch in his voice, I hear him say, "You won't lose us, Elizabeth. Never. After all, you are our fairy godmother."

CHAPTER TWENTY-TWO

Repercussions

I CANNOT GET to sleep Sunday night. I pace about, anxiously awaiting word of the arrival of Lilith and Duke at Sue's *château*. I have eaten nothing, except some chocolate *crèmes* from a box Jean-Luc had given me as an arrival present. By now, they are pretty stale but I don't notice.

Finally! The call comes near 11:00 o'clock from Sue, that the two lovebirds are safely with her and how charming they are and again, it's the most exciting adventure she's had in what seems like forever.

Sue is living virtually alone in the *château*, with only Fabienne, her loyal friend and assistant. On a small stipend from the noble family, an income from the sale of soy products, (the land around the *château* is planted with soy bushes,) and the receipts from opening the property to tours in the summer, Sue is not rich. But what she has, she gives, a woman with an enormous heart.

"You are a true *amie*, Sue," I say, near tears of relief. "Thank God they are with you."

"I must say, the two of them – they're adorable," she says softly. "I am just feeding them some spaghetti and sauce, poor things, so hungry." And in a different tone, "there's more cheese over there," I hear her say to the two, then back to me, "I must say, she is a beauty."

"Isn't she? And just as sweet as the outside. Now, about the tickets."

"First thing in the morning. I hope, and they hope, to be out of France within the next day or two. Of course, you and I will be in constant touch. Love you, old friend."

"Love you," and we ring off. I call Brit to let him know that Lilith and Duke are safe with Sue. We say a hazy, romantic goodnight, promising each other that tomorrow night, we will be together, alone, and, at last, I am able to sleep.

Of course, I awake to a whole different ball game.

In the lobby Monday morning about 9:30, the scene is chaotic. First of all, Willie and Jean-Luc are both behind the check-in desk. The salon is filled with breakfasters, voluble, noisy, ready to take on the new day. There are two, new arrivals, trying to check into the hotel. Brigitte is being run ragged with requests for more coffee, more *lait*, more butter, more, more, more.

But most formidable of all in this scene, is the presence of Hamad al-Boudi, standing tall and fierce, in his flowing robes and white head covering, next to the stairwell descending to the basement, the first place Lilith had hidden many months ago. (Of course, he doesn't know that.) Ahmed, the bodyguard is beside him.

The sheikh's arms are crossed against his massive chest as he looks on with disgust at the crowded lobby. He glares with venom at Jean-Luc who avoids his gaze at all costs. I stand in the back hall, leading from the office, appalled by the implications in Hamad al-Boudi's stance. He is frightening.

It was bound to happen, this confrontation to come. Where is René Poignal when we need him? Not here, this morning. At least, not yet.

The maelstrom diminishes. The people checking in are sent in the direction of their rooms. Couples, and small groups leave the breakfast table and head for the streets of Paris on a handsome day in May, to enjoy the pleasures, the sights, the food, the scents of the prettiest, leafiest, most walkable city in the world. At the moment, I envy them their escape.

All now is in slow motion. Jean-Luc and Willie sit silently behind the desk. I stand frozen in the hall, but in sight of Hamad al-Boudi. We three culprits are to become his target.

"Monsieur," he says in a booming voice. "My daughter."

"Sir," is Jean-Luc's response. He stands up. Willie remains seated, mute.

Ahmed steps forward boldly. "Hamad al-Boudi speaks little French and little English, as you know. I will speak for him," he says, impaling Jean-Luc with his glance.

"What is his problem?" Jean-Luc asks of Ahmed.

"His daughter has disappeared."

"What do you mean, disappeared?"

"She has not been seen by anyone in the family or in the hotel for three days and four nights."

"My goodness. You should call the police."

"But of course, we have. We have checked hospitals. We have talked to the neighbors across the street. We have discussed her vanishing into thin air with your policeman friend, Poignal. We are…" He starts to sputter.

"I wish I could help," Jean-Luc interjects quickly. But of course, he cannot because he knows nothing of her whereabouts, nor her transformation. It is just as well.

Ahmed spies me in the hall and says aggressively, "And you, Madam. You are known in the past to have lent her your coat so she could go about Paris without her burka."

"Yes," I say. "That's true. But that was months ago," I say, coming forward.

Hamad al-Boudi moves towards me. He really is formidable. I stand my ground. "You know something?" he growls at me. I shake my head 'no' vigorously. "And you…waiter in hotel…you…" He is aiming at Willie.

"I sure you know something. You close to us in suite. You serve family."

Willie stands, head down, speechless.

Then Hamad al-Boudi raises his voice and in a torrent of Arabic, lashes out, I'm sure, with invective and curses, all aimed at Jean-Luc. The words 'Hotel Marcel' are heard from time to time. The menace is real.

"What's he saying," Jean-Luc asks Ahmed as the rant continues.

"You are not getting off the hook – as they say in America. That's what he is saying. The sheikh believes Monsieur Marcel knows exactly where she is. He is positive."

"I don't know. I swear it. This man has no right to threaten me and my hotel." Jean-Luc is livid. His voice is raised.

It is at this moment that René Poignal enters.

Instead of diffusing the situation, the detective's presence seems to infuriate Hamad al-Boudi. "You!" the sheikh yells. "What do you do to find my daughter?"

"Sir, we are working on it." René is forthright and unafraid. "Paris is a complicated city. I have my best men combing the area. She can't have gotten far."

"Three days, policeman. Three days!"

Ahmed chimes in, "Even her intended, Saud al-Alami, is angry. He is worried. He has his men looking for her too."

I'll just bet he is upset. His intended – little Lilith – is now tarnished material, or could be, and perhaps even not to be trusted.

Somehow, René manages to walk the sheikh and Ahmed back toward the entrance door of the hotel, reassuring them as best he can, that he is working full time on the situation, that he will inform them immediately with any information as to her location.

René, also, is making it crystal clear that the threats thrown around at the Hotel Marcel and at Jean-Luc's person will not be tolerated, that the sheikh will be formally sent back to Qatar should he act on any such threats, and that the French government is aware of all the nuances of the case.

It's over. For the moment.

CHAPTER TWENTY-THREE

Quelles Allées et Venues

RENÉ RETURNS TO the check-in desk. "*Mon Dieu,* Jean-Luc," he says, "That is some angry fellow!"

"I almost feel sorry for him," I exclaim.

René shoots me a hard look. "Now, why, Madame Elizabeth? Just why should one feel sorry for him."

"He has lost a daughter," I say, meekly.

René pauses, scrutinizing me intensely. "Perhaps you have some secret knowledge?" he says, suspiciously.

"No," I say. "Not really."

He comes towards me as I stand in the hall. "Madame, I feel you are keeping things from me. That is not a good idea."

"Of course it's not a good idea. However, *gentilhommes,* I must leave you now. I have an appointment. I'm already late," and with a wave goodbye, I reach the street quite breathless.

Of course, I have no appointment, but I need to flee interrogation. It is hard to lie, hard to cover up. Do I feel guilty? I guess I do.

A little.

I go around the corner to the rue Cler. It is a wide street of shops lining each side; a small *parfumerie*, a luggage shop, several *bistros*, a *rôtisserie* with chickens turning, a bakeshop in front of which is an outdoor *crêpe* machine. I purchase and devour a warm *crêpe*, loaded with butter and sugar, standing there in the sunlight, thinking of nothing but the sweetness on my tongue. I order a second *crêpe au sucre*.

I go back to the Hotel Marcel. The lobby is empty, Brigitte at the desk. Taking my key from her, I slip past Jean-Luc's office and reach the sanctity of my room with a sense of relief.

I nap for a bit until I am awakened by a call from Sue.

"She is writing a letter to her parents," Sue announces. "Duke is helping her. He adores her. It is sweet to behold."

"I know. They are a joy to be around."

"We booked coach tickets to New York for Wednesday morning. It's a split flight from there to Chicago, but I got those reservations too. Tomorrow was all booked, so they'll be here another day. I hope all is under control *chez l'hôtel?*"

"Pretty much," I answer.

"What do you mean, pretty much?" There is alarm in Sue's voice.

"Well, 'big-Daddy' was here this morning, raising hell – but then, what else can he do? He is quite frantic with rage."

"Understandably," Sue says, under her breath. "I suppose it's to be expected."

"You don't mind having them another day?"

"Of course not. They are great fun, each quite fascinating in his/her own way. But, I must ask you, my driver is taking them to de Gaulle on Wednesday – early in the AM. I'm going too. I'll wait until I see their plane take off."

"Sue, you are something else," I say. "I really appreciate that – knowing they are really off – if it all works out," I add tentatively.

"Well, I am almost as invested in this as you are. Can we lunch Wednesday? I'll have her letter. I want to give it to you to take to The Majestic. Is there some way you can get it to the parents?"

I gulp. "Of course. I'll find a way. And yes. Lunch for sure. *Caviar Kaspia?*"

"Where else, sweetheart," and she rings off.

I begin to prepare for my evening with Brit. How I look forward to relaxed, happy moments with the man who delights me so. There are so few days left before my departure. Monday is almost gone, and next Friday, the day I leave, hardly counts. I decide on the classic, black dress and the diamond studs he gave me last New Year's. I know he loves the look.

Near 7:00 o'clock, as I descend to the lobby to wait for Brit, I hear the voice of René Poignal. "How about that!" he is saying as I enter from the little hall. He has just slapped a folded newspaper down on the top of the lobby desk with a splat. Then, leaning over to read from the page of *Le Monde*, in French: "*Le Docteur Guillaume Paxière*, a well-known physician, was personally attacked on an avenue in the 7th arrondissement, last evening (*Dimanche.*) The doctor's nose was broken, and there was an unfortunate blow to the groin, presumably provided by the knee of the attacker. The doctor did not name the person who inflicted these blows. He claimed it was a personal matter."

"The gentleman got his just desserts!" I exclaim, as Jean-Luc, sitting behind the desk chuckles.

"Huh?" René questions, turning to me. "Ah, Madame Elizabeth."

"That means he got what he deserved. By the way, which lady managed to do this? My guess, Sylvie. She's got the weight and the anger," I say, advancing into the lobby.

"Neither," is René's reply. "It was the wronged husband."

"Pierre?" Jean-Luc looks surprised. "I didn't think he had it in him."

"Well, apparently he did. Guillaume Paxière is not pressing charges because he thinks it all too embarrassing."

"How typical!" I exclaim. "He's such a proud, arrogant kind of fellow. It's all about 'how things look.' He wants to be admired for his cool suaveness." I laugh. "Too late now."

Jean-Luc asks the detective, "How is the widow, Sylvie, taking it?"

"Not too well," the policeman replies with a sly grin. "Not well at all. In fact, she's furious."

"She must want to kill Pierre Frontenac," I remark.

"*Au contraire*," says René. "She's ready to kill the doctor!"

Brit arrives at the Hotel Marcel, just as René moves back to Jean-Luc's office to continue discussing the various problems facing the street where we live.

Brit and I want a quiet moment, away from the hum of lovers and weddings and adulterers, the sound of a ranting voice in Arabic, the clip of scissors, the hysterics of a certain widow, and the pain of an offending doctor. It has been too much.

With all my feelings for Brit, there has always been, until now, a question at the back of my mind, of his trustworthiness. The history of the loss, by suicide, of his former lover, the artist-mate who he had loved, has haunted me from time to time, a strange and mysterious happening that has seemed unreal. However, I have always known that to love is to risk.

It's worth it, the risk. And these last dramatic days have proven to me the steadfast support and involvement of which he is capable. I view his integrity, his dedication to his art, and frankly, his love for me, with a new respect.

"Tonight, something simple," I say, as I take his arm. We walk to the old Peugeot. It is an especially sweet night, the air light upon our faces, my bare arms in the black, silk dress I wear, caressed by the gentle breeze. The car windows are open, and we move beside the Seine at a languorous pace, speaking little, yet much aware of each other.

We decide on a seafood *bistro* on a *quai* beside the river. Over *langoustine* in a buttery sauce, a sublime white *Sancerre*, Brit begins to speak of our future. It comes completely naturally.

"I want to be with you Elizabeth," is his opening remark. "I have never been more positive in my feelings. Somehow, somewhere, we belong together."

"I feel that too," I respond, "but, and I don't want to be negative, you know we have agreed marriage is not an option. I am not young."

"Neither am I," he says with a laugh.

"Even living together on some sort of permanent basis," I continue, "it's perhaps not a good idea. Oh, I love your plan to come and stay with me on Long Island this summer. In fact, I can't wait. But for the long haul, we both need our separate space, our separate OLD habits," I say with a grin, "now don't we?"

And his answer, said with a broad smile, "No wonder I love you."

This evening, after a tumultuous day, ends in the most loving, serene moments at his townhouse in the Marais district on the second floor, our own *vie en rose*.

CHAPTER TWENTY-FOUR

Crime d'Incendie?

WHEN BRIT DROPS me off at Hotel Marcel on Tuesday morning, I see Jean-Luc and Willie Blakely, huddled together in deep conversation behind the lobby desk. As I approach, they look up, and I am struck by the look of consternation on each face.

"What is it?" I ask, concerned.

Jean-Luc pauses. "It's serious, Madame Elizabeth. Come back to my office."

Willie accompanies us, having recruited Brigitte to man the front desk, busy as she is with breakfasters.

Jean-Luc closes the door. I sit on the empty chair. He goes to his post behind the cluttered table with papers, account books, a small computer, and sits down with a sigh. Willie stands leaning against the closed door.

"There is a problem, Elizabeth. You know, Willie, here, is now sleeping regularly in the down-stairs bedroom – the one I created in the basement for emergencies. Every morning early, about dawn, he goes for a little walk, his 'constitutional,' he calls it, after his shower. He locks

99

the hotel front door and ambles up to the corner and down past The Majestic, always with his eye on the Hotel Marcel."

"Yes," I say, curious.

"Well, this morning, in passing the alley between my hotel and The Majestic – you know the passageway where we leave out the trash for pickup by the street cleaners – well, he saw, as he passed, that there was a large black garbage bag covering what looked like a lump, right Willie?"

"A lump?" I say.

"I didna' know at first what I was looking at," Willie begins. "It was such a lumpy tangle on the ground I seen, at the back of the alley near the trash basket where the street cleaners come to pick up. I was mighty curious – even thought it might be a body under there. I go back, very cautiously, and underneath the black plastic, I find a large tin of gasoline, some straw, and a tangle of rolled up paper."

"It seems strange it was right next to the back kitchen door of this hotel. If someone waits there, and the minute the door opens to put trash outside, which Brigitte does on a regular basis…" Jean-Luc says soberly. It seems he cannot finish the thought.

"This is hard to believe," I say helplessly. "I don't understand. Why? What in heaven for?"

"I presume, arson," Jean-Luc says in a loud voice. The word reverberates.

"Arson!" I am appalled.

"Yes. I can only think that someone placed that gasoline there so that, at a given point, when Brigitte opens the door from the kitchen, he can force the straw and paper inside, doused with gasoline and light it."

"Good lord! Have you called the police? Called René?"

"Of course. The first thing I did when Willie told me. He's on his way."

As he says these words, there is a tap on the door. Willie opens it to greet René Poignal, who enters, his face serious.

"*Eh bien*, Monsieur Marcel," he says, standing directly in front of Jean-Luc, sitting behind his desk. "*C'est quelquechose, n'est ce pas?*"

"I'm truly worried."

"But of course," says René. "On my way here, I looked back there – and indeed, there is a tin of gasoline. A large tin – and papers, straw, all ignitable things – just as Willie, here, said –all twisted together."

"Isn't this rather crude?" I ask.

"Crude, yes, but smart," the detective says. "If a detonator or an electric contraption were to be found, it would be much easier to prove arson. But a simple gasoline tin and some straw…well, that would make it harder to prove. In any case, a conflagration, with just a match with straw and gasoline, could bring down the whole hotel."

"*Mon Dieu!*" Jean-Luc looks sick.

"Oh, don't worry too much, *mon ami*," René says kindly. "One of my men is now on constant watch. And I think I know who the culprit is. I have noticed in the last day or two, Ahmed, that Arab bodyguard for the sheikh – well, he's been lurking around."

"Did you actually see him back there?" I ask.

"No, nor did we see him placing the straw and gas tin, but he has not been very cautious in his movements. In fact, he is pretty *maladroit*."

"Clumsy?" I say.

"I guess that's your word. *Gauche*."

"Not a very smart bloke," Willie interjects.

Jean-Luc laughs a little laugh, his despair broken. "Well, we just have to prevent this *crime* or this," and he waves his hand about the room, "this could all go up in smoke!"

"We'll catch him, Jean-Luc. Don't worry." René is resolute.

"I presume the sheikh, Hamad al-Boudi, is behind this," I say.

Both René and Jean-Luc nod. Willie exclaims, "Who else. That Arab man's angry! Blimey. He could commit murder."

"Don't exaggerate, Willie," I say, uncomfortable.

"He lost his daughter, Missus. That'd make a certain kinda man go off the edge."

"When's the next trash pick-up?" I inquire.

"Thursday evening. Oh, Lord!" Jean-Luc is troubled. "What do we do now, René?"

"We wait. We watch. I expect to be here all night because the perp," and he glances at me, proud of his Americanism, "the perp might not bother to wait for Brigitte to put out the trash. He might just break down the door."

And let the fun begin.

CHAPTER TWENTY-FIVE

The letter

I SPEND THE night with Brit. I am no fool.

On returning Wednesday morning to the Hotel Marcel, I find it has not burned to the ground, but Jean-Luc, Willie, and René are creeping around the place quietly, very much present in the situation, and prepared for the worst.

I am unnerved by the whole possibility, which I blurt out to Sue the minute she sits down on the banquette at *Caviar Kaspia*, where we had arranged to meet. "Hamad al-Boudi is beside himself. He's capable of anything, apparently, even arson!"

"This is deadly serious, isn't it?" Sue remarks, summoning the waiter who takes our order. The best beluga. It's my last opportunity to be with Sue, this time around. What other way to celebrate than with caviar, and ice-cold vodka.

"Perhaps this will help," Sue says, reaching in her bag, pulling forth an envelope, and handing it to me. "You know I just dropped Lilith and

Duke off at de Gaulle. I saw the plane they were on take off. They are really gone, my dear."

Sue sees my eyes are glistening with tears.

"They really are such a special young couple," she continues. "The envelope contains a letter to Hamad al Boudi and his wife, from Lilith. I was not privileged to read it, but I understand that their daughter tells them that she is off to America, with a kind benefactor, for them not to worry..."

"Fat chance!" I exclaim.

"I know, but at least there is contact. Maybe Hamad what's his name will calm down. Lilith said that she told her parents she will contact them as soon as she can."

"That's all she said about Duke, that he was a 'kind benefactor'?"

"No. I'm sure she said more, but I _am_ certain she didn't mention they were going to Chicago. That would have been a big mistake, knowing the power of her father." Sue takes a sip of vodka. "Of course, the note is all in Arabic," she says with a sly smile.

"You looked?"

"Of course. Wouldn't you?"

I have to laugh and we toast each other with our tiny glasses of vodka.

"The big chore now is getting this letter to the sheikh, what's his name?"

"Hamad al-Boudi. It's written right there on the envelope."

"Oh, so it is," Sue says. "You'll have to get it to him somehow."

"Me?"

"Who else?" Sue looks surprised.

"But he knows me," I fumble. "He's seen me – certainly his bodyguards have – and Nelson, the manager of The Majestic, he has seen me often. They will connect me, and that means the Hotel Marcel. No, Sue it's impossible." I pause and look her directly in the eye, "But they don't know you!"

"You want me to deliver it?"

"That's a great idea," I say. "With your driver, you go to the hotel Majestic, enter right into the lobby and leave the envelope with Nelson at the front desk."

Sue pauses. "I guess I can do that."

"And Sue, you most act your most regal self, your most Marquise-like. Nelson is such a snob."

"And of course, I won't give my name. I'll just say 'For Hamad al-Boudi, from the Countess'. How about that? Lovely intrigue. Great fun. Oh goody," she says, delighted with her role in the drama.

And this is the way it happens, the way in which Hamad al-Boudi and his wife discover the fate of their daughter Lilith. Sue and I are driven to the street of the two hotels by her chauffeur. I remove myself from the car at the corner of the avenue.

I watch as my friend descends from the vehicle and walks into the lobby of The Majestic.

I wait on the corner, smoke a cigarette nervously, until Sue emerges from The Majestic entrance. She looks so elegant in her chic linen suit of an amber color and a saucy black hat.

Sue turns and smiles at me. She makes a signal of a circle with thumb and forefinger of her right hand, indicating the delivery was successful.

Then she throws me a kiss, enters the car and is driven away into the traffic, headed back to her *château* in Montoire.

CHAPTER TWENTY-SIX

Dénouement

WHEN I AWAKE on Thursday morning, there is the smell of damp smoke in the air, a wet, soggy odor that cannot be denied. Fire! Yet I hear no ruckus, no sirens. I feel no heat.

I had decided, after my previous night with Brit at his townhouse in the Marais, that I was safe enough at Hotel Marcel because of René and Jean-Luc and Willie Blakely. Brit had reassured me, tenderly, and in fact, had determined to stay with me in my little room with its balcony to save me from a conflagration should one happen.

So here we are, two together, aware of the aroma, but safely in each other's arms.

I disentangle myself and go out on the balcony, wrapped in the terry cloth robe. The street is singularly quiet, and although that awful smell is in the air, Paris is Paris on a day in May and nothing seems amiss.

As I glance down on the avenue, I see a couple coming towards me from the right, on the other side of the street. The two are walking arm in arm, upright, vigorous, presenting quite a proud appearance. I realize that it is Pierre and Elise Frontenac, out on a morning walk. They pass, purposeful in their steps, animated, relating, and I am astonished how Elise gazes at her husband. What is it? Is it pride? Is she proud of him, that he smashed the beastly face of Paxière? Why I believe she is!

"We have to go down and find out what happened," I hear Brit say, in a low voice, from the bedroom.

"Of course, of course. Right now."

After dressing, down we go, me in the *ascenseur*, he on the stairs. In the lobby, I see a beaming Willie behind the desk. Jean-Luc's office door is closed, but as I go past, I can hear voices inside. The breakfast salon is quite crowded already, but before we go in to sit there, I stop and ask Willie, "What happened?"

He puts his finger to his lips. "A tiny fire," he whispers, "quickly put out and Ahmed with handcuffs round his wrists!"

"No!" I whisper back.

"I'll tell ye more later," and Brit and I make our way into the salon and find two empty chairs.

The usual plenteous breakfast repast is presented and devoured by Brit and me. The table clears itself of customers who are off and running towards the day ahead. Finally, as we drink the last of the *cafés au lait*, the room is quiet. Jean-Luc and René have come up to the front desk and are quietly conferring with Willie.

"Monsieur," I call, "and detective?"

"Ah, Madame," says Jean-Luc, moving to join us. René lingers with Willie for a moment, then, he too, sits at the table with us.

"There was a fire?" I ask.

René nods his head. He looks tired. "Yes, but we caught it - and him - in the act!"

"Tell us what happened," Brit says.

"It was close to midnight, last night," René starts. "I was here, in the kitchen, having a *café*, when I heard the sound of the door lock being tampered with. It's a very particular sound – of scratching and metal against metal, very specific. I did nothing at first, but stood directly next to the door, gun drawn."

"It sounds like a movie!" I exclaim.

This obviously pleases René who continues, "the noise at the lock ceased, and I heard the distinct sound of liquid being poured and of a match striking and then the crackle of flame! With that, I threw open the door, which opens outward, knocking over the man – Ahmed – just as he's trying to shove unlit paper, pushing the flaming paper, into the kitchen."

"I still think it's awfully crude," I say with a little laugh.

"*Peut-être*, Madame, crude but lethal," he responds soberly.

"Of course," I say, properly admonished.

"This is no joke, Madame," René continues. "This is classic arson."

"Then what?" Brit says, leaning forward.

"It all came together after that," Jean-Luc remarks. "René called me. I came over from across the street immediately. René, here, and his man on the street, they had doused the fire with water. It was quite large, wasn't it?" he says, turning to the policeman.

"Yes. The area was *considérable*, oh, maybe ten, fifteen meters, but it was put out quickly so no real damage was done. And the culprit was in custody."

"Bravo!" Brit says.

"Whew!" I exclaim. "What happens to Ahmed?"

"He is in the jail. He, of course, will try for extradition to Qatar. He'll probably get it because no real harm was actually done."

"And Hamad al-Boudi? He was surely behind this?" Brit asks.

"The sheikh has been asked – no told – to quit France and go back where he came from."

"Will Hamad accept that?" I question.

"*Absolument!*" René exclaims. "I warned him of extremely unpleasant publicity if he did not comply. But I imagine he will employ Interpol to try to retrieve his daughter?"

"Oh, God," I say.

"So, it is over, eh, René? At least for the moment?" Jean-Luc announces.

"Only after the sheikh is gone," he answers. "Only after he has left the country. He is expected to leave tomorrow. Then I can rest."

I sit in silence, savoring the moment, yet realize that Hamad al-Boudi and I are leaving on the same day! Tomorrow! Is his private plane parked at de Gaulle? Will we run into one another?

Well, I think philosophically, what will be, will be.

"By the way, René," I say, changing the subject and mood, "I saw Elise and Pierre Frontenac on the street today. They looked quite happy. In fact, he looked quite puffed up."

"I believe they are quite content, Madame, with Paxière out of the picture."

"He's really out for good?"

"Indeed," says René, with a broad smile. "The gentleman has moved on – probably to another avenue where a lady of two will take his fancy, and he will have his fill."

"You really think it's over for Elise?" I say, feeling a bit nosy, but I can't help it.

"Yes. I do think it is *fini* for her. I happened to interview Henriette, you know, their *femme de ménage*. She was very positive, said much between the two has improved." Then, with a sly wink, he continues, "according to Henriette they are now sharing the same bedroom once again."

"*Bien*," Brit chimes in. "*Très bien*."

And we all laugh.

"It sounds good to me," I say, looking at Brit.

"Me too!" is his response. He rises to leave. "I'd best be going. You know, work to do, paintings to paint, life to be lived," and he leans down to kiss me lightly.

"Tomorrow night, Brit? Dinner with Elizabeth and Isabella and me?" Jean-Luc asks, rising from his chair.

"*La soirée dernière*, for the moment," I say sorrowfully.

"We'll be there," Brit replies to Jean-Luc. Then, with a consoling kiss, he moves from me into the lobby and out.

Before going upstairs to begin organizing my packing, I corner René, who is about to leave. "Can I ask you something?"

"*Mais, oui*, Madame Elizabeth. Anything," he says with a smile.

"It's about Sylvie. Sylvie LaGrange. How is she? She is not my favorite person, but she must be upset about the doctor, no? I've noticed that the blinds of her apartment are always drawn."

René gives a little laugh. "Upset? That's not the word. *Hystérique!*"

"Hysterical?"

"*Bien sûr.* There is no other word. It got so bad that another *docteur* has been attending her. He is much younger than Paxière, but then, the widow does not seem to mind. You know Sylvie. *La veuve joyeuse.* She will survive."

Apparently, in more ways than one.

CHAPTER TWENTY-SEVEN

A Last Supper

I SPEND MOST of Thursday in my room, preparing for the flight home. I pack carefully, placing the folder with Brit's charcoal drawing of Lilith, with her long black hair, (the 'before' picture) between two shirts in the center of my suitcase.

Around noon, I decide to go around the corner to *Le Nôtre* to get the requisite number of macaroon-presents for particular friends at home who have come to expect them. I also pick up a *salade de crevettes*, from the cold case at the shop for my lunch.

Jean-Luc has told me that he has made dinner reservations at the tiny restaurant, close by, *Bellehara*, for 7:30, that Brit and I are to come to the apartment across the street around 6:00 for *un apéritif*, and that we would proceed from there.

After my excellent *salade* and warm shower, wrapped in terrycloth, I lie down upon the bed briefly. Lilith is on my mind. After viewing her drawing again, so lovely in its perspective, so light and ethereal a vision, I can only pray for the two young ones. Should I warn them of Interpol?

Could that agency possibly lay hands on her and return her to Qatar? I would think not. First, they'd have to find her, and, after all, it would be kidnapping.

Rising, I go out on the balcony. Indeed, Sylvie's damask drapes are pulled, her blinds closed to the outside world, on this an especially soft and gentle spring afternoon, the light shadowing as evening approaches. The leaves of the trees that line the avenue never appeared more green, and the scent of the city which is distinct and layered, piques the nostrils, as does no other scent in the world. Paris.

Tonight, I wear a white dress, sleeveless, diamond studs in my ear lobes. I carry a pale pink cashmere sweater, and as the phone rings to announce the arrival of Brit in the lobby downstairs, I run to the door, run to the *ascenseur*, run toward love.

At Jean-Luc's apartment, the champagne is cold, the roasted nuts warm, and the *Brie* melting on its croutons. Sasha and Ray Guild are there, just for drinks, but I am glad because they are both such a part of my life in Paris. The ambiance is rich with emotion.

Tonight is a night of good-byes – at least short good-byes, I hope, God willing. We speak of the last, past days; of the escaped lovers, of the angry sheikh, of the unhappy Croix *ménage*, of Louise's passion to rebuy Jean-Luc's home, of the widow, Sylvie, with her *crise de nerfs*, of the reconciled Frontenacs, of Willie and his plethora of skills, of Rashid, the new fashion designer, now much in vogue, and very much to be a part of the magazine, *Vogue*, according to Ray, with his 'modest Muslim' designs.

Sasha is praised for his underworld connections, making it possible for Lilith to own a new passport. He plans a new book of *Façades*, this time, in of all places, the capital city of Qatar, Doha.

"No!" I exclaim.

"I think Arab architecture will be of enormous interest – just as the Arab mode of dress is bleeding into the juices of Paris *couture*. Instead of a war of civilizations, how about a blending of cultures!"

"You're right," I say, "as usual."

"I don't know about 'usual'," Sasha responds, "but in this, I think I'm correct. Of course, not all things blend easily, like the grand hotel, The Majestic!"

"You are right again," Jean-Luc, says firmly. "I think that place will never be...how do you say...*assimilé?* The Majestic and Hotel Marcel are still at war. We will remain that way for a while. After all, one of their clients tried to burn down my hotel!"

"Hard to forgive," mutters Sasha.

"Impossible to forgive!" Jean-Luc exclaims.

On this more sober note, Sasha and Ray leave us to dine together elsewhere, saying effusive goodbyes, with hugs and kisses, and *à bientôts*,

We gather our belongings and prepare to quit the apartment. Brit and I take one last look at his painting of The Eiffel Tower, the perspective from underneath, looking up. It brings tears to my eyes. All I can think of is Lilith clinging to the cold metal of that structure, with her bare toes in the snow on the ground.

The restaurant, *Bellehara,* is a miniature place, with a small window on the street and no more than eight tables inside, dressed in white linen cloths, and silver utensils. The owner/chef greets us with enthusiasm. Jean-Luc has ordered for me in advance the entrée, *ris de veau,* grilled sweetbreads, a craving of mine that is classic but hard to find. This I find particularly endearing in my host, to remember how fond I am of the dish.

Champagne is ordered, as is, for a first course, the pea soup, probably the most exquisite soup I have ever put in my mouth. The tiny French peas are in season right now. There is nothing that can touch their sweetness. Laced with cream, *la soupe des petits pois* is matchless.

As are the *ris de veau!* Crisp, delicate, soft inside, I devour them unabashedly. "*Quel diner!*" I exclaim. "It is unbeatable."

I can see Jean-Luc is pleased by my enthusiasm.

We are quiet at dinner. So much has been said. So little more to say, except perhaps goodbye. And that we do, walking back to Hotel Marcel. Again hugs, kisses, the world of *au revoir, adieu, bonne chance – tous les mots de partir.*

In the lobby of Hotel Marcel, I find Willie. I thank him for all his helpfulness, his kindness. He looks at me with a tear in his eye, and in his growly, cockney voice says, "It's been a real pleasure, Missus. It's been grand to make yer acquaintance." And I leave for the bed upstairs, Brit tromping quickly up the stairs as the elevator rises.

It is our last night, at least for the next two months, when, after separation, we can come together as we do this night.

On Friday morning, it is Mounir, my Moroccan driver, alone with me in the van taking me to the airport. I leave Brit in my room on the fifth floor. Before going downstairs, after my suitcase and carry-on have descended solo in the *ascenseur*, I step out on the balcony to take one long, last look at the theater of the three apartments across the street. They are all closed and silent.

But not next door. The entrance to The Majestic is alive with activity. There are three limousines waiting in front on the avenue. The one in the lead is a white stretch beast, twice the size of the other two black vehicles. I see luggage, bodyguards, (no Ahmed!) two ladies in full burka, glamorous paper bags of purchases, with the names of the *couturiers* emblazoned upon them, Dior, Yves St. Laurent, Rashid, L'Oreal, Victoria's Secret, quite a load to take home to Qatar. It is an amazing display.

Finally, the tall, massive, berobed Hamad al-Boudi appears in all his glory. His step is fast and furious, but his head is lowered, and he moves as quickly as possible toward the white limo, ready to fly away from the scene of what he concerns a crime, to the sands of Qatar and his luxurious life there, daughterless.

As the *entourage* enters the flow of traffic, I slowly return to my room.

Brit is there, in my bed, his hair tousled against the pillow. He holds out his arms, and I am enclosed in them for a brief moment, before pulling away, running my hands through that hair, then kissing him deeply.

"Goodbye, my darling, for now. Next stop, Long Island!"

"Long Island," he says with a broad smile, and I leave my love in bed with a dream of the summer to come.

It's not a bad way to leave Paris, if one has to leave the City of Light and love, not bad at all.

EPILOGUE

THERE IS ONLY one small hotel for me in Paris. It represents love and life and all things French to me. As I sit on the plane from de Gaulle, heading back to the roar of New York. I remember the joys and sorrows and drama the small hotel has given me. I can only thank the small hotel, 'creep into my little shell', and in my mind, stand upon the balcony off my fifth floor bedroom, and view Paris with fresh eyes, as I do every time I'm there.

I have come there often. I will always come there, as long as life permits me to. This past visit – three weeks of constant affection, excitement, with characters larger than life, love affairs consummated, hysterics in full volume, adulterers punished, and fires set, I have decided that is just the way it is at my small hotel, a microcosm of an emotional world that I crave; it is just the way the *macaron* happens to crumble, *chez L'Hôtel Marcel.*

And how tasty it is!

I have Duke Davis' Chicago address in my purse. I have Lilith's 'before' drawing by Brit in my suitcase to send to the two lovers. I have my love's promise to be in Long Island with me for a long, hot summer.

I have Jean-Luc's and Isabella's wedding in my book of memories, with Brit's unusual painting of The Eiffel Tower on the wall of their new apartment. I have the picture in my mind of Elise, finally smiling up at her husband, Pierre, with pride as she clutches his arm. I have the mental vision of Doctor Guillaume Paxière with a broken nose and bloodied ego.

And Sylvie? I can only imagine the plight of this poor woman behind the shuttered windows of her apartment in building 3. She is surely one of the most vituperative personalities in all of Paris, although, I don't know. *Parisiennes* are notably *dramatiques!* Who knows, for Sylvie, a new, young *docteur/amant?*

And Willie. Willie Blakely. What a fellow! A new and cherished personage in the roster of Hotel Marcel inhabitants. Without his sweet machinations, a Duke/Lilith combine could never have happened. It is his skill as a barber, a waiter, as a loyal, caring creature that has made for even the hope of a future for the two young lovers.

Then, there's Sue, my Marquise, the 'Countess' who delivered the *coup de grâce* to Hamad al-Boudi and his frozen wife with the net result of Ahmed in cuffs and a conflagration thwarted. 'Oh, goody', as Sue is fond of saying. What spirit she has, and what affection I feel!

Sasha? There is always Sasha. Thank God for his picture-taking attributes, and his connections with forgers, making possible the passport to heaven (Chicago?)) for Lilith. And Ray Guild, in the background of all the goings on, with his irony and wit.

Thinking of all these treasures, I feel sleepy and rest my head against the small pillow provided, even on a day flight, by Delta Airlines. It has all been too good to be true, and as I doze off, I can't help singing myself to slumber with the Rodgers and Hart song, softly in my head, "There's a small hotel, with a wishing well, I wish that I was there...forever."

À Paris, tous est possible.

DEDICATION

THERE IS ONLY one person to whom I dedicate this fourth and final book in the "Hotel" series: Jean-Marc Eber.

His small hotel, *L'Hôtel Eber-Mars*, on the avenue de la Bourdonnais in the 7th *arrondissement* of Paris, has been the site and inspiration for all four adventures I envisioned. It is a place where the city of Paris seems to reside, and allows one to dream a life not found elsewhere, if only for a few days.

Jean-Marc. *L'Hôtel Eber-Mars* is timeless, indestructible.

Thank you.

ACKNOWLEDGEMENTS

THERE ARE SEVERAL to acknowledge for assistance in producing the "Hotel" series.

First, Nichole Karr, who took the photograph used on the covers of all four books. It was taken from the balcony of my room on the fifth floor of *L'Hôtel Eber-Mars*.

Second, Todd Engel, Engel Creative, who designed the covers.

Third, and most significant, Marcia Rosen, Literary Representative, who assisted me in numerous ways; editing, encouragement, marketing.

To all, I am grateful.

CPSIA information can be obtained at www.ICGtesting.com
Printed in the USA
LVOW04*2326200315

431459LV00002B/3/P